THE SACRED BULLOCK
AND OTHER STORIES OF ANIMALS

When autumn came he led him to fairs and advertised him for sale
(*see page* 114)

THE
SACRED BULLOCK
AND OTHER
STORIES OF ANIMALS

BY

MAZO DE LA ROCHE

ILLUSTRATED BY
STUART TRESILIAN

TORONTO: THE MACMILLAN COMPANY OF
CANADA LIMITED, AT ST. MARTIN'S HOUSE

1939

ALS CONN! CG097347-1

661526
S.F.

COPYRIGHT

51

PRINTED IN GREAT BRITAIN
BY R. & R. CLARK, LIMITED, EDINBURGH

CONTENTS

THE SACRED BULLOCK

"HOI! Hoi!" Young Davey shouted, as he and the dog which was a mixture of several breeds and combined the intelligence of all of them, drove the little bullocks along the rocky path toward the pasture where they were to be fattened for market.

"Hoi! Hoi!" he shouted, even when it was not necessary, for he liked the sound of his own voice in the desolate place, and his brain was so empty that a single world like "hoi" meant much to it.

The great barren hills, in the heart of Wales, that seemed to have upheaved themselves from the bowels of the earth, might have been expected to have dwarfed the figure of a man driving a dozen bullocks before him, with a dog at his heels, but they did not. He, in his heavy boots, thick corduroys, with his broad shoulders and plunging walk, looked massive, towering above the little beasts he drove like some powerful prehistoric man. On their part they looked soft and weak, their sturdy legs not yet accustomed to the rough paths, their eyes timid, as they looked over their shoulders at the dog.

Beyond and beyond, the hills reared their rocky heads, their shoulders shaggy with bracken. Beyond and beyond, they crouched and sank like receding waves. There was always the endless variety and endless monotony of the hills. Up and up the morning sun showed its face among them, lifting their veils of mist, casting their dim shadows into the valleys. In the most fertile of the valleys was the farm where young Davey worked. From this height you could see its stone walls and its two chimneys. He looked down at it and, for a moment, the faces of the two who lived there came into his mind. Then it was empty again and he shouted " hoi, hoi ! " to the bullocks and drove them along the path.

The two who lived there were a farmer named Owen and his daughter Glennys. Twenty years ago Owen had come home from the War, blinded. He had married the girl who had been waiting for him and, two years later, she had died in giving birth to his daughter. All these years he had been worked for, waited on by a married couple but last summer the husband had strained his back. It was little he would be able to do for a long while, so young Davey came from a distant farm to help. He was so strapping, so willing that Owen liked the sound of him about the place. He asked Glennys to tell him what the boy looked like.

" I wish you could see him," said Glennys, laughing, " he's a funny-looking boy ! "

" Ugly to look at ? "

" Well, not exactly but he has a thick neck and a high head and he has tow-coloured hair in curls on the top of his head and his eyelashes are almost white."

" He sounds ugly and not a bit like a Welshman."

" Oh, he's Welsh ! " laughed Glennys. " He can't speak a word of English."

" I like his voice," said Owen. " I wish he spoke oftener. And I like the sound of his step."

Young Davey slept in an attic room under a roof that sloped to the floor. There was nothing but a bed in the room and an old iron-bound chest for his clothes. He owned a quite good coat which he wore when he went to church but the heels were always out of his socks. He owned a Bible in very fine print but he could not read. He washed himself in a shed at the back of the house. All his life he had washed with coarse yellow soap but now Glennys gave him a piece of pink soap with a scent to it. It had only cost tuppence but to him it seemed luxurious and he was careful not to be extravagant with it.

He was happy as he drove the little bullocks along the track. He shouted " hoi, hoi ! " loudly and felt the strength of his power over them as they ran and stumbled, not knowing what they were expected to do. Far below he saw the farm-house, looking very grey and small. Then his mind returned to the bullocks which were to be fattened for the market and he called to the dog to harry them up the path to the pasture.

The pasture lay on a plateau against the side of a ruined Abbey. Owen had had the piece of sheltered rich land fenced in and the grass grew thick and strong here. A protecting hill rose on the north and the walls of the Abbey kept off the cold east wind. It was said that in olden times the monks had their garden here and that a richness had been left in the soil that would for ever nourish what grew there.

" Hoi ! Hoi ! " Davey shouted at the little beasts and they crowded in at the gate, looking with frightened eyes at the dog who just touched their legs with his teeth.

There was one bullock that was not so obedient as the others. He turned and faced Davey with a wondering look and lowered his head, with its little coral pink bumps of horn, toward the dog. Davey had noticed him before and now he had a good look at him.

He was white, with a peculiar milky whiteness above his pink skin. The others were red, or red with a patch of white. But he was white all over and it gave him a look of purity and innocent power. There was a bunch of white curls on his crown, rather like

4

Davey's. His tail ended in a white ringlet. Only his great liquid eyes that seemed to see but a short way, were of a midnight blue.

"Hoi!" shouted Davey. "Hoi!" and waved his staff.

The dog barked sharp orders at the bullock. It wheeled and went after the others.

Davey could not keep his eyes off it. As it bent its massive little head to graze he stood staring at it, admiring it. It was shy but not timid. He filled his hand with its curly topknot, ran his hands over its silky sides, appraised it for the good beef it would put on to its sturdy frame. It stretched its neck, its wet pink nose following his fingers, its under-lip thrust out in its instinct for sucking.

The bullocks had been bought by Owen for fattening. Twice a week he asked Davey how they were getting on.

"They're putting on the fat wonderful," said Davey. "There's a white one."

"Oh. Is he a good one?"

Davey laughed. "He's the best. He looks like a regular little——" He could not talk for laughing because Glennys was in the room and the sight of her filled him with confusion.

Christmas was past. It was January and a misty sunlight, not without warmth in it, slanted across the hills. Owen said:

"I think I'll go up the path and see the beasts."

"He can't see them," thought Davey. "He means feel them." And he chuckled to himself.

" All right, Father," said Glennys. " Shall we go now ? Davey could come with us, couldn't you, Davey ? "

She looked so beautiful to him, standing in the dim room, with the fairness of her skin and the darkness of her hair and her large grey eyes, that his legs felt heavy and his head light. He twisted his fingers together and looked at her from under his white lashes, not able to speak.

Owen was on his feet, groping for the peg where his cap hung. He did not like being helped, so the boy and girl watched while he found it and put it on his head. He led the way through the door and along the cobbled path. At the end of it he stopped and threw up his head.

" What's that I smell ? " he asked.

" Snowdrops," said Glennys. " It's wonderful how you can smell them, Father. Their scent is so faint."

Owen smiled proudly. It filled him with pride to do some things better than other people could. Glennys picked a few of the flowers and put them into his hand. He laid his other hand on her arm.

Davey led the way up the steep rough path, up and up, his strong legs springing before them, the rags dangling from his coat, the dog pressing close after him. He was so eager to show off the bullocks that he could scarcely endure to wait for Owen's slower steps. The sheep grazing on the hillside moved closer to each other, for they seldom saw so many people. A faint baa came from their midst. It came from the

6

first lamb of the season who stood, peering between the bodies of the sheep, that were a woolly barrier between him and the world.

" 'Tis a new lamb," said Davey. " The ewe dropped it yesterday. There'll be more before sundown."

The lamb cried out again, his close curled wool shaking with the strength of his baa. Suddenly he dived under his mother and bunted the milk from her udder with his curly head. His cry had gone through Owen with the piercing sweetness of the first voices of spring.

" I wish I could see the lamb," he said.

Glennys led him on up the path. The ruin of the Abbey rose before them, the broken arch of grey stone, the crumbling tower solid against the fragility of the wintry blue sky. Through the windows Glennys saw the little bullocks grazing in what had been the chapel.

The bullocks raised their heads and stared meditatively through the windows at the group approaching. Then, as though with calculated design, they passed through the narrow door of the chancel into the open pasture — all but one.

This was the white bullock and he stood motionless on the delicately carved altar-stone that had fallen and now lay sunk in the grass.

" Oh, lovely ! " cried Glennys. " Doesn't he look lovely there ? "

" Who ? Where ? " demanded Owen, turning his face impatiently from side to side.

" The white bullock. He's like the sacred bull of pagan times. The sacrificial bull."

" Is he getting fat ? " asked Owen.

" He's best of them all," said Davey. He was smiling in pride because of the girl's surprise. He strode to the bullock and grasped him by the curly topknot and drew him toward Owen. He came docilely, stepping daintily over the grass, but his eyes were two luminous globes turning in courage and pride.

Owen passed his hands over him. " What a silky hide ! " he said. " Yes, he's putting on the flesh."

" What a pity he has to be killed ! " said Glennys. " He looks so lovely here. I'd like to keep him. . . . He looks sacred."

" You're a foolish girl," said Owen, pressing her arm against his side.

" The beast should be saved for breeding," muttered Davey in Owen's ear.

" Hmph, well, he just came with the lot I bought. Take me to the others."

They passed through the door and found the little herd in a russet clump among the bracken. The white bullock followed them. Even when they were far down the path he stood staring after them. He watched their movements contemplatively till they were out of his sight. Then he returned to his companions but never seemed entirely to belong to them.

The remembrance of the visit Glennys had paid to the ruin was always coming into Davey's mind.

" She got a surprise, she did ! " he would chuckle, and he would wonder if ever she would come to see the bullock again. He would pull and push him till he got him on the altar stone, then he would stand gazing at him in wonder and admiration.

The bullock soon learned that he was singled out for attention but he scarcely had to learn it, for he was not timid like the others. He watched for Davey's comings and pressed forward to get the hay he spread on the ground or to thrust his nose first into the bucket of meal. Davey would lead him into the chancel and strew his share on the altar because that was where he had stood on the day Glennys had praised him.

One day she showed Davey a picture in an old book of a sacred bull. His horns rose out of a chaplet of flowers and young girls and youths, in Greek dress that showed their lovely limbs, danced in procession after him. They had musical instruments in their hands and vine leaves in their hair. Davey had never seen a book like this before. He took it reverently and, as he looked from the picture to her face and back again, a smile lighted his face and a tremor ran through him. He asked, in his Welsh tongue :

" Was there really times like that — in the world once ? "

" Of course there were ! "

" I wish I'd lived then."

" Oh, Davey, you would have looked funny among the Greeks ! " Then her eyes swept him appraisingly and she added : " Well, from the neck

9

down, you'd have looked all right. Yes, the Greek tunic would have suited you."

He did not understand but he stared at the picture, trying to draw sense from it. He was ashamed of the fervour of feeling that swept over him. A rich colour rose from his neck and flooded his boyish cheeks.

"I'm going to sew a patch on your coat," said Glennys, "and darn your socks."

He looked at her, startled by the fervour in him. He pushed the book into her hands and clattered up the stairs to his attic. From the chest he took his clean pair of socks that had both heels worn through, and hid them under the mattress of his bed. He found pins and pinned up the tear on his sleeve. "She'll not mend for me whatever," he said, the tears filling his eyes.

But, when he hung the coat on a peg in the kitchen while he cleaned out the stable, she took it down and mended the tear and when he next looked in the chest there were the socks folded together, with neat darns on the heels. He held the socks to his breast and his heart throbbed like an engine against them.

He could not thank her but, when they met in the passage, he said :

"You'd ought to come and see the white bullock, how he's growing."

"So I should," she answered, her face bright in the dim passage. "I'll come to-day."

"Do you think your father will come too ? " he asked timidly.

"No. He's tired. He's been out all the morning. I shall come alone."

She saw the muscles about his mouth quiver and his eyes turn away, as though he was afraid to let her see into them. She had a sudden feeling of power. Yet the power was tremulous with something strange. Ought I to go alone with Davey ? she wondered. It may seem too familiar. Yet surely I can go to look at my father's beasts when he can't see them himself !

As they passed through the garden he said :

" You ought to bring some flowers to make the bullock one of them things — what you said — for his head."

Glennys laughed. " Davey, you are romantic ! "

" What's that ? "

" Oh, having pretty ideas about flowers and old-time customs and all that."

" We could take some daffydils."

" We shall do no such thing."

She spoke a little sharply and there was silence between them as they mounted the steep path. But the March wind was so sportive and so scented with new growth, the clouds were so white and so flowing that, before they reached the plateau, they were laughing into each other's eyes for joy in the little lambs that played all about them.

The lambs were strewn over the hillside, white and weak and gay. They broke into sudden sidewise darts. They flung out their woolly legs in an abandon of play. Forehead to forehead they tried their infant strength against each other. The sheep watched them with no maternal pride, no responsive gaiety. Their cold eyes and flat pale cheeks were bent toward the grass and they forgot that they ever had been lambs.

The white bullock was not with the others that came to meet Davey.

" Where is the white bullock ? " Glennys asked.

" You wait and see."

He led her into the Abbey and there, standing on the altar-stone, was the massive little beast, his eyes luminous for the feed that would be strewn there, his hoof gently pawing the stone.

" I've never seen anything like it ! " cried Glennys. " It's wonderful ! Have you bewitched him, Davey, or has he bewitched you ? "

" Hoi ! Hoi ! " shouted Davey to the bullock, and he strewed a little meal on the altar-stone.

" How clean and white he is ! " she said.

" I brush him. He's like that beast in the picture you showed me. He's sacred."

" But he's for the market."

" Don't tell your father how he thrives, will you ? I'd like to keep him a little longer."

Glennys felt troubled as she looked at Davey standing there in his strength and his ignorance. He was like the white bullock. He was aloof and belonged to another age. They were like the lonely hills and the wind-swept stones of the Abbey. She went to the beast's side and laid her hand on his shoulder. He swung his head on his thick neck to touch her with his tongue. She saw how his little horns were growing so that they arched above his curly pate, smooth and sharp and threatening. But his eyes were gentle, she thought. As she looked into their blue-black depths, she saw no intelligence there, just an overwhelming instinct.

" Isn't it strange," she said, " how the monks once lived here ? Do you ever think of them, Davey, and imagine what their life was like ? "

" Monks ! " he said. " Who were they ? "

" Don't tell me that you haven't heard of the monks who built the Abbey ? "

" I haven't heard." He looked at her dumbly, his hands clasping the smooth sickle of the bullock's horn, and she noticed how luminous his eyes were and the pulse that beat in his strong neck.

" The monks built the Abbey seven hundred years ago. They built it for worship."

" Worship ? "

" Yes. Worship of God and prayer. That part out there, where the other bullocks are grazing, was the cloister."

" Did the monks live alone here ? Without women ? "

" Yes. They were holy men."

" Touch me," he said, moving closer to her. " Lay your hand on me — like on the bullock."

She spoke to him in a high clear voice :

" How did you think the Abbey came to be here ? "

" I thought it had always been."

" But it had to be *built* ! "

" Put your hand on me." He came still closer. " Like on the bullock." She could see the white glimmer of his skin under his shirt.

She turned pale and moved quickly away from him.

"I made a mistake, coming up here with you," she said.

The bullock moved through the space between them and pressed through the narrow priests' door into the cloisters among the others. Glennys turned her back, trembling with fear, and walked swiftly out of the ruin. But Davey did not follow her. He stood looking after her through the broken arch of a window, till she was only a midget decending into the valley. Then he followed the bullock and laid his mouth against the place where her hand had lain on the animal's side. Tears fell from his eyes and he sought to make something clear, that he might understand, out of the confusion in his mind.

Spring had come too soon. Now, in the middle of March, winter came back for a space. The hills turned savage and bleak. The snow came down in thick flakes and was blown in drifts against the iron of the hills. When the young lambs saw it falling they knew it for their enemy and ran out bravely to meet it, stamping on it with their little hoofs, flattening the flakes into the ground. But the lambs were weak. They could not stamp all day long and, after a while, they crept under the warmth of their mothers' wool and huddled there.

The ewes watched the snow coming down for two days, standing close together, their cold eyes without apprehension or compassion for their lambs. Then they sank to their knees and the drifts began to bury them. Davey worked all day shovelling them out of the snow, dragging them up to their feet. The sweat poured from him and he took a slab of bread and cheese from his pocket and eat it, leaning on his spade.

The Sacred Bullock

That night the snow came down harder than ever. Davey did not wait for daylight but was out of bed in the bitter cold dawn, staring through the leaded panes of the attic into the terrible white fortifications of the hills.

Glennys had not spoken to him since the scene in the ruin but now he clumped in his hobnailed boots to her door and rapped.

" If the sheep are to be saved," he said, " you must come and help me."

" I'll come at once," she answered.

" What is the matter ? " shouted Owen from his room.

" It's the snow ! " she called back. " I must go with Davey to help with the sheep."

" Oh, curse this sciatica of mine ! " cried Owen. " I should be going too ! "

" Don't worry, Father. We shall save them."

With a scarf wrapped round her head and neck she plodded up the hill after Davey, placing her feet in the holes his feet had made in the snow. He carried the two spades and she a basket with sandwiches in it and a thermos of cocoa. He felt a fire of strength in him as he struggled upward, knowing she was close behind. He leaped through the drifts, eager to show off his strength.

A great mound marked where the sheep huddled. Davey and Glennys ran to it and began frantically to dig. The sheep were uncovered, stretched on their sides, their pale tongues lolling, their white eyelashes motionless over their pale eyes. Sometimes they lay heaped on top of each other. Then the ones at the bottom were dead. Most of the lambs lay dead, some

15

with noses close to the ewes' udders. There had been more than thirty lambs. Now there were just three. Davey dragged the living sheep to their feet and supported them but they gave him no look of gratitude, or pleasure at the lambs that lived, or pity for the ones that were dead. They stood humbly, gently, waiting for the life to come back into them.

" Don't cry so," said Davey.

" I can't help it," answered Glennys. " The lambs were so sweet." She was holding the weakest of the three living ones in her arms. He was the only black one and his little black face lay on her breast. She was so hot that she had thrown back the scarf and her fine hair clung to her head in a dark mass.

Davey looked at her kneeling there in the snow and his mind was clouded and dark, like the sky overhead. His speech came thickly.

" Stop your crying and pull your scarf on your head. You'll take cold."

She smiled a little at the authority of his words. She dried her eyes on the corner of her scarf but she did not cover her head.

" I'm so hot," she said, " I should die if I covered my head."

Davey threw down his spade and strode to her. Before she could stop him he took her scarf in his hands and drew it close over her head.

" You shall keep your hair covered ! " he said thickly. As he returned to his digging, he kept on saying : " You shall keep it covered. You shall . . ."

They worked in silence then, digging out the sheep.

The black lamb's dam was dead and no living ewe would suckle it. Perhaps it was because of its colour but, weak as they were, they gave pale hatred to it out of their eyes and would not let down their milk.

At last Glennys was so tired that the spade fell from her hands. The sweat trickled down her face.

" You stop digging and drink some cocoa," said Davey. " I can finish the job. Look at the sun. There's a change coming."

A mildness was in the air. In one place, like a tunnel in the clouds, the pale sun peered through. A breeze stole up from the south. The black lamb's fleece began to curl closely.

" Yes, I must rest for a bit," she said. " My back aches. Look ! The sun is really coming out."

" Rest in the stable," Davey said. " It's nice in there."

" The stable ? "

He pointed, with his spade, to the ruin. " I call that the stable."

She laughed. It was the first time she had laughed that day and, when he saw her white teeth and her lips parted and the escaped black lock on her forehead, he felt the joy of her nearness almost unbearable.

She thought : " If he follows me into the Abbey I will go out at the other side. I will not be alone with him in there." With the lamb in her arms she went through the snow which was not so deep on the plateau, into the Abbey. Here it was sheltered and the sun poured between the delicate stone arches and filled the ruin with an ethereal beauty.

Glennys laid the lamb on her skirt. She unwrapped the scarf from her head and covered the lamb with it. She had found a corner with clean straw in it and she laid her food on the carved top of a fallen column. She did not let her mind dwell on the sheep and lambs that had died but on those that had been saved. She wet her finger in the cocoa and the lamb beside her sucked it.

Then she saw the bullock appear in the narrow doorway that opened into the chancel. He stood looking in at her, the crescents of his horns bent above his curly poll, his forelegs thick and short beneath the bulk of his strong breast.

He stood staring at her in surprise. She could hear the breath blowing in his wide nostrils. He pressed through the door and she wondered if she ought to be afraid of him. There was the lamb's little head, showing above the scarf. Perhaps the bullock had it in his mind to harm the lamb.

He came closer. His glowing yet senseless eyes moved insolently in their sockets. His coat glistened, the long hair silky like fur. He stared at her and at the lamb. Now she gave a loud clear scream and struck at him with her fist.

Davey came leaping through the snow. He shouted :

" Don't be afraid ! He means no harm. Look now, he does just what I tell him ! "

But the bullock pushed Davey aside with his shoulder and thrust his wet nostrils against the girl's breast. " He means no harm ! " shouted Davey and caught him by the horns and swung him away.

Glennys watched the two of them wrestling together. Whether there was anger or just mischief in the bullock, she could not tell. Now he swung Davey from side to side, as though he would hurl him off. Now Davey bent the beast's proud neck and pushed him closer to the door. Now he had the upper hand. The bullock was thrust outside the Abbey. A heavy wooden bar closed the entrance.

Davey was laughing but his breath came in harsh gasps. He dropped to his knees beside Glennys. " It's a pity he frightened ye," he said, " for he means no harm."

" I wasn't frightened," she answered, " except for the lamb. That was why I screamed for you."

His love poured from his eyes and she began to rise but he put out his hand and held her by the skirt. " Hold me," he said, " like you did the lamb. Hold me in your arms."

Glennys tore herself from him and ran out of the Abbey. She ran through the deep snow down the hillside, putting her feet into the holes made by his. " How dared he ! I hate him ! I hate him ! " she said over and over again. Yet her anger was so mixed with love that she could not tell one from the other.

After a while Davey carried the lamb into the kitchen. He said gruffly :

" Is the lamb to die, or will you feed it ? "

" I have warm milk in a bottle, waiting for it," she answered gently.

She took the lamb from him and laid it on the warm hearth. " Oh, pretty, pretty, pretty ! " she whispered to it, and it sucked from the bottle with all its might.

Its body warm, its stomach full of warm milk, it soon began to totter about the kitchen, putting its pert face into every corner and, as it felt its strength return, gambolling as it would in a meadow.

Before long Owen sent for a cattle buyer to look at the bullocks. He needed money for his season's work. But, on the morning, Davey told him that one of the bullocks, the white one it was, should be held back for a little. It had been struck by a stone falling from the tower of the Abbey and hadn't thrived for a bit, but it would be all right.

Owen told the drover to have a look at it, in any case. But it was not with the others and Davey said that it was shut in the stable.

" What stable ? " asked the drover.

" Oh, a stable," answered Davey, vaguely. " He isn't ready for killing yet."

When the eleven red bullocks had been herded away, Davey let down the bar and the white bullock stepped out of the chancel, in his pride and his beauty. He raised his head toward the April sky and the round white clouds that drifted across it were not whiter than he.

Now Davey had him all to himself. The hills stretched, wave upon wave, hump upon hump, to the horizon and, on this hill, he and the white bullock alone together. Davey did not ask himself why he loved the beast, why the thought of him being butchered was more than he could bear. He did not ask himself why he doted on his beauty and fed him delicately and kept fresh straw for him to lie on. In some mysterious way the beast now bore the burden of Davey's love for Glennys. Davey would put both arms about him and press his forehead to the place where her hand had lain.

But, since their bout of wrestling, the bullock was not so docile as he had been. Now, when Davey approached, he swung his tail and pawed the tender grass. There was a challenge in his eyes, even while he did what he was bid. He was restless, always moving in and out of the Abbey, throwing up his head and distending his nostrils against the wind. He seemed to be always expecting some fresh service from Davey. He did not move sedately, as the other bullocks had, but with force and arrogance.

Owen kept asking about him and Davey always said : " He's better, but not fit for killing."

Davey had grown sullen and scarcely looked at Glennys. But she looked at him more and more often.

The farm labourer whose back had been strained was now well and able to work. Owen paid off Davey and told him he could go.

" This is the end of it all," thought Davey, in the chaos of his mind. From the garden he stole spring flowers and carried them to the ruin of the Abbey. With his thick hands he made them into a wreath and placed it on the bullock's head.

" Now," he said, " you are like the sacred bull in the picture. . . ."

Davey was to leave the farm that day but when

evening came he had not returned to the house for his box, which stood packed, waiting on the doorstep.

" Wherever can the boy be ? " asked Owen, again and again.

Suddenly Glennys said she would go and look for him.

" Let the man go," said Owen.

" No, Father, I shall go myself ! "

She climbed the hill, in the golden evening light. In the Abbey, on the altar-stone, she found Davey lying dead. Near by the white bullock was quietly grazing. The crescents of his horns rose above a chaplet of spring flowers and the points of his horns were red with blood.

ELECTRIC STORM

I

MISS MINTON thought she had never experienced worse heat than this, and she knew a good deal about heat. When she had first come to Canada from her native Lancashire she had spent several years on the Western prairie. She had seen the parched land crack for the lack of moisture. She had seen cattle die for lack of food because drought and heat had killed the grass. She had seen the prairie bleached to nothingness.

Yet, standing in the doorway of her cottage on this August afternoon, she said aloud, though she was alone except for her cats :

" I have never felt anything like it ! "

Probably she was wrong. The natives of this well-wooded corner of Ontario, with the great lake lapping its shore, would have said that she did not know what she was talking about, that she was deliberately giving the place a bad name, that she was crazy. As she was talking to herself, they would have inclined toward the last belief.

She was far too gentle to have argued with them, but as there was no one there to contradict her she repeated :

" I've never felt anything like it ! It's enough to kill a cat, isn't it, Timmie ? "

Timmie was a tawny yellow Persian cat, thirteen years old, with a flat, inscrutable, angry face. As a kitten her disposition had been spoiled and she had never got over it, though she had been comforted, petted, fed on her favourite foods for six years, by Miss Minton. It was certain that Timmie's yellow eyes were always looking for trouble, and generally finding it.

She had been given to Miss Minton, rather against Miss Minton's will. But she had no power of resistance where animals were concerned. Indeed she had little power of resistance where the desires of people were concerned, having spent a great part of her life in nursing relatives and friends through illnesses, looking after their children when they died, undertaking, without protest, tasks that were too heavy for her.

Not that she was spiritless. On the contrary, she had very good spirits, and, when it came to endurance and making the best of a bad job, she had a quite remarkable courage.

She had two blessings which she was always thankful for. She had work she loved and congenial companionship. The work was weaving, the companionship cats.

She earned her living by weaving, which she did on an enormous old loom brought from Newfoundland. It quite filled her little living-room, overshadowing all else.

Sometimes it seemed to her like an instrument she could play on. It hummed and throbbed and even sang to her. Yet, unlike the songs of other instruments, its music did not die on the air, but was captured, held fast, in the colours and textures of the stuffs she wove.

In truth Miss Minton had the soul of an artist.

Now, as she turned from the doorway and cast her eyes over the work she had done that day, she saw to her dismay that she had captured something of the sultry August heat and woven it into the scarf she was making.

Surely that threatening purple, that sulphuric yellow streak, were not a part of her original design! Surely the patron who had ordered this scarf would be dissatisfied and it would remain on her hands, unsold!

She decided that she did not much care. She liked the scarf. The weaving of it had helped her to endure the crushing heat. Now the sun was burning its way towards the west. Before many hours the relief of the evening would come. Then she and the cats would stroll together in the moonlight. She would give them something special for their supper. Their saucers of milk stood untouched, soured by the heat.

Before she sat down at the loom she went to see what the thermometer, hanging beside the window, registered. The mercury just touched 102 degrees. There was not a breath of air. The vine outside the window hung limp and lifeless. She pressed her fingers on the earth of the potted fern and found that it was still moist. The fern bore up well.

She placed herself on the seat before the loom and began to work the treadles. The low humming sound soothed her nerves. She smiled at the three cats because they were watching her so closely. Three pairs of eyes glowed at her and there was a different expression in each pair. Timmie's looked angry and yet amused, as though she had a rather sinister joke up her sleeve. Patchy's eyes were pleading, and Ali's bewildered and a little frightened.

Timmie was in her favourite seat on top of the loom. From this point she could see all that was going on, both outside the door and in the room, even while she appeared to keep her gaze fixed on Miss Minton's deftly moving hands. Patchy sat in the rocking chair, from where she could look down into the box in which the kitten lay curled in a close yellow ball. It was a week old.

Ali sat on the window ledge. It was through this window that he made all his exits and entrances. In a sense, he was the outsider, for he never had kittens.

He was Timmie's grandson and bore a spurious resemblance to her, being twice removed from the Persian.

The habit of having kittens was so firmly fixed in Timmie that her thirteen years had yet scarcely hampered her. She had them several times a year, always tawny like herself, always of weaker physique. She was still strong, though she had gone through many an illness, in addition to the bearing of kittens.

Disposing of Timmie's kittens had, in the past six years, been one of the chief problems of Miss Minton's life. There was also the disposal of Patchy's kittens to vex her.

The kittens were all so sweet, yet everyone in the neighbourhood, and even beyond the neighbourhood, had been supplied. The drowning of kittens hung over Miss Minton like a cloud ; whenever she saw the bodies of Timmie and Patchy beginning to swell and sag the thought came, with a pang of pain, " More kittens to find homes for ! What if I can't do it ? What if they must all be drowned ? "

There had been drownings lately. Miss Minton and Timmie and Patchy had been having a very bad time. Just a week ago Timmie had had kittens. The one comfort about it was that her litters were growing smaller. There were not so many kittens to dispose of. In the last litter there had been only three. Two of them had to be drowned and the third now lay curled in the box, not minding the heat at all. A good home had been found for it when it was older. Miss Minton thanked goodness for that.

Two days after Timmie had had her kittens Patchy had given birth to four. No one had wanted them, so they were all drowned. The drowning was made as easy as possible for Miss Minton by the good-natured Finn who occupied the other half of the cottage. But nothing could make drowning easy for the kittens. The day it was done Miss Minton had sat at her loom with tears streaming down her cheeks, and her emotion had turned a quite gay scarf she was making into a sombre one. One kitten left out of seven ! It was hard — it was hard !

The problem of Patchy's bereaved heart had been mercifully solved. A few hours after her kittens were born Timmie had picked up her own kitten and leaped with it into the box beside Patchy. When Patchy's four kittens were destroyed the two mothers had attended to the one remaining kitten with thoroughness and mutual content. There was peace in the cottage. It was only Miss Minton who now and then gave a thought to the little lost lives.

Then suddenly, the day before yesterday, Patchy had turned against Ali. She was his aunt. What relation he was to the various litters of kittens was a mystery, even to the cats. But his manner disclaimed all connection with them.

He had come into the room with his usual slinking, apologetic air, when Patchy, with a scream that had gone right through Miss Minton, leaped from the kitten's box and flung herself at him. He had fled from the room horrified.

Whatever was in Patchy's mind against Ali she

had been able to communicate to Timmie. When evening came and he stole fearfully home, first Patchy had flung herself at him shrieking, then Timmie had descended on him from the top of the loom, with a still more savage yell.

The noise had been so terrible that the Finn and his wife had run from their side of the cottage to see what was the matter. He had suggested that the remaining kitten might be the bone of contention and that perhaps he had better drown it. With her dark blue eyes flashing, her small head with its mass of iron-grey hair erect, Miss Minton had almost driven him from the room. Indeed, in that moment she had got rid of feelings she had harboured against the Finns. Good-natured as the Finns were, their nearness was a trial to her, their noise, their litter, their never-ceasing foreign talk that penetrated through the thin partitions. She blamed herself for feeling resentful toward them. They were kind neighbours and she could always depend on him to — oh, why did the thought of drowning kittens return so painfully to her mind?

The heat had, it seemed, softened the bitterness of both grandmother and aunt toward Ali. That day he had gone in and out of the cottage unmolested. Now they did not even glance at him as he sat on the window ledge. He kept his eyes fixed on the strip of flypaper that dangled from the ceiling, where a score of flies buzzed their death song. His long thin tail, in contrast to the thick fluffy tails of his aunt and grandmother, occasionally twitched.

Miss Minton found it hard to move the treadles. The power seemed to have gone out of her legs, but she worked on. The scarf she was weaving showed an almost sinister individuality. She did not feel able to control it. The eyes of all three cats closed. They dozed to the humming of the loom. The kitten, which had never yet seen the light, curled itself in deep primeval slumber.

II

Sunset brought little relief from the heat except that the impersonal glare of the sun was gone. With it went any stir of air that had enlivened the day. There seemed nothing to breathe.

Miss Minton felt that she wanted a good drink of cold water more than anything on earth. She took a tin pail from the bench in the kitchen and set out. There was no water supply in the cottage. She had to carry it from the neighbour's well, excepting the rain water which she caught from the eaves. But there had been no rain for weeks.

She had to cross a field to get to the well. The cats followed her, Ali keeping in the rear, now and again uttering a soundless mew. The corn in the field stood harsh and dry, ants scurried on the sandy soil and locusts chirped their thin dry song.

Miss Minton pumped and pumped, seeking the cold water at the bottom of the well. Some of the water splashed over her feet and the cool moisture pleased her. Then she remembered that drought had made the water low and that she must not waste it.

She filled her pail. The cats lapped the pool on the pump stand.

In her kitchen she drank long from the shining tin dipper. She felt refreshed, but the thick hair hung heavy and moist on her forehead. She remembered that she had promised the cats a special treat for their supper. It must be a tin of salmon.

There was just enough in the tin for the three of them. She gave the most generous portion to the females because of all they had been through lately, eking out Ali's portion with some cold rice, of which he was very fond. He waited till Timmie and Patchy

33

were eating before he approached Miss Minton. His mouth was open in an apologetic smile.

All three attacked the fish with avidity, making hissing noises as they drew it into their mouths. The very smell of it in such weather was almost too much for Miss Minton. She made herself a pot of tea and ate a few biscuits.

She had hoped for a moonlit evening, but now remembered that the moon would not rise till after midnight. She went down the path and sat on the grass a little distance from the cottage, for she felt that she could not talk to her neighbours. They were sitting on their verandah, the man smoking, the woman peeling apples for apple sauce.

The quick dusk had already fallen, but no dew. A mood of playfulness had descended on the cats. They darted about her, peering at each other through the long grass. Even Ali ventured to join in the play. But he was wary.

Miss Minton had brought the kitten in the crook of her arm so that it might breathe the air. It seemed to her that she could not remember the time when there was not a kitten to curl in the crook of her arm. Now and again it stretched its tiny legs and she felt its claws, as fine as the finest fishbones.

Heat lightning played on the horizon, and as the evening drew on there were rumbles of distant thunder. Perhaps a storm would come and cool the air. Perhaps there would be rain! She pictured how the rain would soak into the parched earth, how refreshed all living things would be by it.

At last she called the cats and went slowly back to the cottage. Her neighbours had gone to bed and it was very quiet. The tall pines that stood at either end of the cottage loomed darker than the dark sky. She had always liked these trees, but often felt them to be a danger.

The cottage seemed even more breathlessly hot than it had during the day. It stood, as an island of heat, in the sea of night. She felt that she should like to sleep on the verandah, but she was sure a storm was coming up and her tired body longed for the ease of her bed. She locked the screen door, returned the kitten to its box, and made ready for the night. Ali leaped to his place on the window ledge and peered out. Timmie and Patchy got into the box with the kitten and both made as though to nurse it. It stretched between them, in the heat of their furry bodies, and at last discovered a teat. Miss Minton could not tell which cat the teat belonged to, but she heard a contented purring from them both.

III

Miss Minton was woken from a heavy sleep by something moving about her. She was not as startled as some might be, for occasionally one of the cats took it into its head to sleep on her bed. But there was something different in this. The cat walked the length of the bed making soft trilling noises in its throat, talking, without doubt, to the kitten. In another moment the kitten was introduced under the edge of the sheet against Miss Minton's neck. It pressed its tiny claws into her and mewed faintly.

" Oh, naughty, naughty ! " said Miss Minton. "Which of you two has done this ? " She turned on the light and saw Timmie standing on the side of the bed looking angry and roguish and pleased with herself.

" It cannot be," said Miss Minton. " I cannot have the kitten in bed with me. I might roll on it and smother it. Besides — well, Timmie, you ought to know better."

She got up and carried the kitten back to its box. Patchy was lolling there with arms open for it. Miss Minton laid the kitten on Patchy's breast and it scrambled there, hunting for a teat. Timmie leaped into the box also. Ali was curled up in the rocking-chair.

When the light was out and she was back in bed Miss Minton had a glimpse of her room in a vivid flash of lightning. There was an angry flourish to this lightning very different from what she had seen earlier in the night. She would be glad of a storm if it brought plenty of rain. She kept her thoughts quiet and again fell asleep.

She was dreaming of rain in an English garden. She was trying to discover whose garden it was and why she herself was in it when she was again woken by one of the cats walking over her. She was instantly tense, almost alarmed. She put out her hand to feel which cat it was. She put one of her hands right on the kitten, held in the cat's mouth. Miss Minton ran her hands over the cat's sides and knew her to be Patchy. The fur was less long and fine than Timmie's. She exclaimed : —

"Whatever have you in your silly minds to-night ? You are making me angry, do you know that ? And making me lose my sleep, which I need ! "

She got out of bed and turned on the light. Patchy dived under the sheet and deposited the kitten there.

Miss Minton carried the kitten back to the box, Patchy following, purring loudly. Timmie lolled on her back, arms spread to welcome the kitten. Miss Minton laid it on Timmie's breast. It meowed feebly. Patchy sprang in beside them. Ali had left the chair and was sitting on the loom. He stared at the strip of flypaper that dangled from the ceiling just as though he had never left off staring at it.

Miss Minton went back to bed.

There was almost continual lightning now, and a small faint breeze that rustled the dry needles of the pine above the cottage. Miss Minton felt it on her face and was thankful. She lay a while listening for thunder, but it did not come. Again she fell asleep.

But her mind was disturbed. She never ceased dreaming. Now she was back in the prairie province. She could see the prairies stretching on and on to the horizon, feel the hot wind that swept across them.

Almost before the cat was on the bed she was awake. She was angry with it, yet she had to laugh. It was so ridiculous, this bringing of the kitten to her bed. She wished she had not taken off the door and substituted a woven curtain. Then she might have

37

shut herself in. This time it was Timmie who brought the kitten.

The next time it was Patchy.

The next time it was Timmie.

The next time it was Timmie again. The breeze was stronger now, and all the boards of the frail cottage were straining as though it were an unseaworthy ship.

Now neither of the cats would get into the box with the kitten. They walked up and down the room, waving their plumed tails, staring with hostile looks at Miss Minton. Ali sat on top of the loom staring at the fly paper. A dead branch of one of the pines was sawing against the roof as though it would saw it in two.

IV

For a long time Miss Minton could not sleep, yet the cats made no attempt to come in to her. She knew that they paced up and down in the outer room, waiting for her to sleep.

When at last the fitful slumber came to her she dreamed that the loom was spinning of itself, humming and turning, turning and humming. Over and over it hummed the words, " The mother-one gave birth to another one. . . . The mother-one gave birth to another one. . . ." For some reason Miss Minton disliked these words very much and felt bitter towards the loom for humming them.

She was woken by a terrible commotion taking place on top of her.

She was so excited that she struck out blindly.

The furry body that her hand encountered leaped to the floor with a scream, then back again to the bed. There was a flash of lightning so steady, so brilliant, that, sitting up wildly, she saw exactly what was going on.

Timmie and Patchy were both on her bed, scrabbling desperately to extract something that had fallen between the mattress and the wall. Their long arms stretched, they pawed and peered, hindering each other, spitting and sneering at each other. It was the poor kitten that was wedged there between bed and wall !

They had thought to force her to submission by coming together ! The one she had struck — she was sure it was Timmie — had given her a nasty scratch on the hand. Blood was oozing through.

" Oh, you bad cats ! You wicked things ! " she cried. She had never spoken to them so before.

She put her hand to her mouth and sucked the wound. She was surprised to find that she was in darkness. What she had seen was vivid in her mind, every hair of the angry cats, their upright bushy tails, their glowing eyes. " Dear heaven," she thought, " the kitten may be dead ! "

She sprang from the bed and turned on the light.

The cats saw that she had taken the situation in hand. They withdrew composedly to the foot of the bed. She stood a moment irresolute, afraid to draw the bed from the wall, afraid to see the limp, smothered body of the kitten.

All air seemed gone from the room, as though the night had sucked it out to add to the approaching storm. The hands of her little clock on the dressing-table pointed to three. She counted three drops of blood on the back of her hand.

" One, two, three," she counted aloud, and, as though the storm had been waiting for this signal from her, a shattering clap of thunder burst from the sky.

Miss Minton screamed in terror and put her hands to her horrified ears. The two cats simultaneously leaped straight into the air, then again stood rigid, staring at her. An attenuated whisper of a mew came from the kitten. It was alive ! Miss Minton drew the bed from the wall a little way, put down her hand and rescued it.

Its fur was in wet tufts from so much carrying about and pawing. It opened its pink mouth and curled its tiny tongue.

" Dear little kitty ! " she breathed, snuggling it.

Now came a shrill whistling sound of wind. Forked lightning split open the sky, which clapped itself together again in consternation.

" This time," said Miss Minton, " I shall put you both in the box with the kitten and cover you up, so you can't get out. Why didn't I think of that before ? "

She laid the kitten in the box, then ran about closing windows. Rain was beginning to lash against the walls. She wondered about Ali, then saw him sitting on the rocking-chair peering into the box at the kitten. The rocking-chair swayed slightly.

She was struggling with the stiff latch of the kitchen window when she heard screeches of rage from the mother cats. The screeches seemed ripped from their innermost being. She ran back to the living-room.

Timmie and Patchy stood by the kitten's box, their lips drawn from their pointed teeth, every hair on end, their tails lashing in rage. Ali was in the box with the kitten. . . .

Whether some latent bond between him and the new-born creature was stirred to life by the storm, whether male curiosity concerning the activities of the females had got the better of him, or whether some perverse desire to enrage them had given him courage for this, could only be guessed at. He peered up at them with his half-sneering, half-apologetic look. The kitten crawled over his lean breast searching vainly for succour.

Simultaneously with a flash of lightning that discovered the outside world in livid detail, his grandmother and his aunt leaped on him. The box became a whirlpool of writhing tawny bodies, their shrieks mingled with the sharp crackle of thunder.

In and out of the whirlpool the kitten's body appeared, helpless as a leaf on Niagara. Miss Minton was brave, but she dared not put her hand into that box. She stood petrified, her small oval face very pale, waiting for the moment when she might help.

Suddenly Ali shot from the box and tore like a yellow streak around the room, the she-cats after him. The kitten was hurled to the floor. It lifted its face from side to side like a blind worm.

Ali fled to the bedroom. Miss Minton had a glimpse of the three speeding across the bed.

They came out again, and for a space ran head to tail in a frenzied circle. Even Ali's tail looked bushy. He was panic personified. He fled to the kitchen and Miss Minton heard the overturn of the pail of water from the bench. When they reappeared Ali's fur clung to him in wet tufts.

He sprang on to the rocking-chair and from there to the top of the loom. The three ran across the top of the loom like a fantastical frieze. Miss Minton heard herself laughing. There was a deafening, splintering crash, as one of the pine trees was struck by lightning.

From the top of the loom Ali described a wide arc toward the door. Miss Minton sprang forward and threw it wide. The three cats shot out into the livid brightness. She shut the door.

She picked up the kitten and held it under her chin. It snuggled weakly there. A thumping came on the wooden partition and the Finn's voice called out, " De beeg tree is bust ! "

With the blasting of the pine the storm had spent its power. First a lull came, then a longer lull, then a gentle silence with a faint patter of rain to break it.

Miss Minton did not wake till nine o'clock. The kitten was still asleep beneath her chin. Sweet cool air and the smell of the refreshed earth filled the cottage.

When she opened the door the three cats entered, Ali behind the others. Each one of them bore some mark of the battle of the night before, but Ali bore the most. Patchy at once leaped into the box beside the kitten and began to nurse it. Timmie leaped after her and began to lick it vigorously. Ali took his place on the window ledge and stared up at the flypaper.

Miss Minton picked up the bottle of fresh milk left by the milkman. All three cats began to purr. First she filled her little milk-jug, then their three saucers. Then she put the kettle on.

An exquisite breeze blew into the cottage. She saw the loom waiting for her, the happy cats lapping. She smiled.

TINY TIM

HE was unaccompanied and he was going out to America as a Christmas present to a young lady. He was nine months old but looked on himself as grown up. His legs were short and straight, his body sensitive, alive, as tense as a fiddle string and he had a square muzzle, a hysterical tail and a black spot over one eye. His pedigree was as long as his days were short.

In England he had been the pet of a young man and an old lady. When one of them was not making much of him, the other was. There was not a corner of the house, from attic to basement kitchen, where he was not welcome. The maids let him kiss them or even bite them if he chose. His kisses were swift, moist licks; his bites mumbling, gnawing, long-drawn-out worryings that left a good deal of slobber but no pain.

But his favourite dream was the way he would have bitten cats, if he could have caught them. He would wake from this dream gnashing his small teeth and spring to his feet and stare about him.

" Cats, is it ? " the old lady would enquire and she would hobble to the door and let him out into the garden. He would rage up and down it, screaming of his desire to catch a cat.

The old lady had been most untidy. Three maids and a tidy grown-up grandson could not keep the house from looking as though it had been stirred up with a spoon. It was an exquisitely happy home for Tiny Tim because, no matter what he did in it, he could never do wrong.

So the first nine months of his life passed and then the untidy old lady died.

Tim missed her a good deal. She had made a delightful cushion to lie on when he was tired from play and she had always been ready to hobble to the door to let him in or out. In fact, letting Tim in or out was the chief excitement of her day. No one else could do it so satisfactorily because the wheeziness of her breath always contributed to Tim's gusto in rushing out or bounding in.

But what he missed most, perhaps, was her untidiness. Now, if he worried the corner of a rug it was soon laid back in place. If he tore the filling out of a cushion, the rent was at once mended and he was rebuked. Old shoes, old bones, which he had loved to keep handy on the drawing-room rug, were taken away where he could not find them. There had always been at least four dishes of food and drink on the floor of the room. Every time he barked at the sugar basin she had given him a lump. He always had the jam spoon to lick. It was useless for her grandson to tell the old lady that Tim would die if she kept on like this. She knew better. She knew that it was she herself who was most likely to die.

So, when she died and the young man was given a post in the East, he decided to send Tim as a Christmas present to a young lady in America. And Tim was to carry all the young man's love with him. Some day, it was hoped, those three would live together.

When Tim found himself in a small cage in a small room on board ship he felt more curious than alarmed. His only companion was an immense Irish wolfhound whose name was Oona and who was accompanied by a grim and silent master. Oona utterly ignored Tim. When they were let out of their cages for exercise, he tried to make up to her at once. It had always been so easy for him to make friends that he thought all he had to do was to stand on his hind legs, put his nose against her muzzle and beam at her out of his hazel eyes. The next moment she would be rolling over and over with him, pawing him quietly, racing with him round and round the room.

But Oona did nothing of the sort. She looked

straight through him with a sombre gaze. She stood as a rock while his small paws padded against her like little waves. But, when he gave her a warm lick with his tongue, she lifted her long velvety lip and snarled.

He made several attempts to win her. He brought his ball and his rubber bone to show her. He got directly in her way, looking up in her face ingratiatingly. But she turned her head away from ball and bone and, when he stood in her path, she stepped over him.

He would stand under her, looking out from between her powerful legs as between pillars, her rough body looming above him like a cloud. He was exquisitely clean and dainty. She was unkempt, strong-smelling. She had an immense attraction for him.

He would sit gazing at her by the hour, nervous shivers running along his spine and through his legs. He never seemed to sit solidly down. His thin little stern hovered shudderingly above the heaving deck.

It was a bad voyage. From the first day out they encountered fog, rough seas, gales. Oona became more and more melancholy. She began by being very sick and, after that, she refused all food but a mouthful or two of dry biscuit. This she would turn over and over in her mouth while Tim watched her in rapt attention ; then sometimes she would spit it out again, turn it over on the floor with an expression of disgust and finally bolt it as though to be rid of the disgusting sight of it.

Tiny Tim

No sort of weather affected Tim's stomach. He crunched his biscuit with his square little muzzle turned up to the face of Grierson, his keeper. He swept the dish clean of his soft meal in three gulps. In between he wondered what had become of the innumerable little snacks he used to enjoy. He wondered what had become of the house where he had romped, the garden where he had chased imaginary cats, the large soft lap where he had snuggled, the two strong young hands that had snatched him up and stroked him or put on his lead or sometimes cuffed him. To do justice to Tim it must be said that he missed the kindly lap, the strong hands, more than the delicious tit-bits.

He was constantly on the look-out for love. Those who came to the kennels were friendly. They scratched him behind the ears sometimes but they were all alike and none of them was like his old lady or his young man.

Oona's master was as unfriendly as Oona herself. Twice daily he took her for a walk. They stalked out, stalked round the deck and stalked back again, without looking in the direction of anyone else.

When Tim saw Oona's lead being snapped to her collar he was wild with excitement, wild to go with her to the deck. He danced about on his toes and filled the air with his pleadings. But he might not have existed as far as Oona and her master were concerned.

Tim had the feeling that if he could go for a walk he might find his old lady or his young man.

49

Sometimes he had such a burden of love in him that he felt he must find somewhere to deposit it. At others he felt strangely full of hate, growling for no reason at all.

But on the third morning something happened. A young man and a young lady, having nothing better to do, came to look at the dogs and decided to take Tim for a walk on deck.

It seemed too good to be true. Tim was *so* frantic when they really set off. He so strained against the collar that he had a fit of coughing and the young couple thought he was going to be sick and all but took him back to the kennels.

His feet scarcely touched the deck. He bounced in an ecstasy of hope. Surely now he might find his own house, his own garden, his own old lady.

But he found none of them. The young couple, whose names were Jean and John, held him so closely on his lead that he became quite tired and ceased to strain. He walked sedately, with wistful looks into the faces of all he met.

Everyone was kind to him and it became the thing for Jean and John to take him for walks. Everyone knew him by name and bits of cake and sweets constantly came his way. Jean usually led him because he was so becoming to her and she held his lead so short that he always felt as though he were about to choke. They often passed Oona and her master, looking gloomier and more aloof as the days went on.

In this new world of Tim's there were only two

dogs, himself and Oona, and Oona would not look at him, would not exchange sniff for sniff or lick for lick. The more he saw of John and Jean the less he liked them. There was no one on board for him to love. He gobbled up all the food that was offered him and grew thinner and thinner. At night he dug into the straw of his cage and tried to dig through the floor itself. He lay curled up in a little shivering heap. He longed to obliterate himself.

Then on his rocking horizon appeared a new old lady. She was even more solid, more impressive, more comfortable than his own old lady. She came up the steps from the tourist class, hanging on firmly to the brass rail, and promenaded solidly around the deck leaning on her ebony stick and peering through windows and doors with an air of dignified curiosity.

One of the deck stewards came up to her apologetically.

" I'm very sorry, Madame," he said, " but this deck is reserved for the cabin passengers."

She stared at him.

" Can't I walk about and look at it ? " she asked.

" I am afraid not," he returned, still more apolo getically.

" Well, well, I'm sorry I have come where I shouldn't but when one is on one's first sea voyage one likes to look about."

" Of course," the steward spoke deferentially. " It's quite natural and I'm very sorry indeed——"

" It's your duty," she interrupted and turned back towards the stairs.

The steward assisted her down them and returning met John with Tim on the lead. They were waiting for Jean.

" Did you see that old lady ? " asked the steward.

" Yes," answered John, without interest.

" Well, she's one of the Mount-Dyce-Mounts."

" One of the Mount-Dyce-Mounts ! " echoed John, unbelievingly.

" Yes, and it's her first trip. She's going out to see a married daughter in British Columbia. Travelling alone. I hated terribly to turn her back off this deck. But I couldn't help it. She's a lovely old lady, she is indeed."

" And a Mount-Dyce-Mount ! " exclaimed John, and forgetting all about Jean he hurried down the steps dragging Tim after him and went up to where the old lady had settled herself in her chair. The sun had come out, the sea calmed and it was fine for the time of year.

John introduced himself, with a charming air, to old Mrs. Mount-Dyce-Mount and begged her to let him know if he could be of the slightest service to her.

She thanked him kindly and was interested in Tim. She patted her lap and he sprang on to it. His nostrils quivered over the stuff of her dress. Then he looked long and earnestly into her face. He swiftly touched her cheek with his tongue. He gave a joyous bark. It seemed too good to be true. He had found another old lady !

He saw a good deal of her, though not half as much as he desired. John took him to the tourist deck to call on her twice every day. If John went without him she asked at once for the little dog. The trouble was that the call was short and what Tim longed to do was to stay close by her side, for ever and ever, as long as this strange heaving world lasted.

When John, knowing that Jean was waiting impatiently for him to play deck tennis with her, dragged Tim away to the kennels, Tim dug his nails into the deck, made his small body rigid and turned up his hazel eyes full of pleading and hate for John.

Once the old lady said : "Do let him stay !" And Tim curled up on her lap for an hour of supremest content. When John came to fetch him Tim snapped at him and, when they were alone together, John hit him with the end of the lead.

There was a fog off Newfoundland. The ship lay motionless in the sullen ice-cold water while all night long the warning whistle sounded. Tim lay curled up tightly, shivering through all his tender being. That day John and Jean had become engaged and they lay awake planning for their future. Old Mrs Mount-Dyce-Mount lay awake too, thinking of the past and dreading the long rail journey to British Columbia and wondering if her daughter-in-law really wanted her.

Towards morning the engines started. All the passengers who were awake gave sighs of relief and thought, "Thank goodness, we're off."

The ship moved through the sullen water very quietly as though feeling her way. But an iceberg submerged in the depths collided with her in a shock so terrible that those who slept were soon awake, wild with fear. A heavy sea was rolling.

The attendant let Tim and Oona out of their cages. Oona was unmoved by the excitement about her but when her master appeared she went to him with a slow wag of the tail and a sombre light in her eyes.

Tim capered over the decks, a new hope possessing him. Perhaps this strange world of the ship was about to disappear and he would find his way back to his own house and garden. He liked the peculiar listing of the deck which the humans found so terrifying. He dug in his little nails, cocked his ears and investigated places where John and Jean had never permitted him to go.

Presently he saw them rushing frantically, hand in hand, their life preservers on askew, Jean's silk pyjamas fluttering in the icy wind. He flew after them barking.

It was not one of those shipwrecks in which people behave with fortitude, though heroic deeds were afterwards recounted in the newspapers. Perhaps there were too many on board like John and Jean, who fought their way hysterically to the best places, not giving a second thought to old Mrs. Mount-Dyce-Mount.

Tim loved the sight of these pyjamaed legs. He had always longed to bite them and now he darted after them nipping first one and then the other. Jean shrieked terribly.

" Oh, oh," she screamed, " he's gone mad ! "

John screamed and kicked out at Tim and shouted : " Somebody kill this dog ! He's gone mad ! "

Women screamed in a new terror and a man un-expectedly whipped out an automatic from his pocket and fired at Tim. The boat listed still more. There was pandemonium aboard.

Tim had not liked the revolver shot at all. He skulked down a stairway and trotted, one ear pricked and the other lopping, along a deserted passage.

He sat down and licked the spot where John had kicked him. Then he scratched and the thumping of his elbow on the floor sounded like an imperative knocking.

" Go away ! " A harsh old voice came from within.

It was the voice of the old lady. Tim was gal-vanised by it into joyous activity. He tore at the door and it swung open. Mrs. Mount-Dyce-Mount was revealed sunk on a seat beneath the closed port-hole which showed nothing beyond but grey-green water. The luggage in the cabin had slid to one side. The toilet articles were on the floor.

Tim saw nothing of this. He only saw his dear old lady and he leaped into her lap and began ecstatic-ally to lick her face, whimpering with joy as he did so.

" Timmie, Timmie, oh, you naughty little boy ! " she murmured, and for a moment she hugged him to her. Then she said, " But you should not have done this. You should not have done this ! "

But Tim thought he should. He began to in-vestigate the cabin. He became even more worked up for he smelled Oona in it. He leaped back into his old friend's lap and informed her with hysterical barkings that Oona had been here.

"But you should not have done it," she repeated. "Poor little Tim, you should not have done it. Perhaps if you go up on deck someone will save you. Go away, now! Naughty boy! Oh, dear, I wish you would go!"

Her voice broke and she began to cry.

Tim curled up in a tight ball and began to shiver from head to tail. But, almost instantly he uncurled and stood tense on the slanting floor, listening. He heard Oona and her master coming. They were creeping cautiously along the passage which was becoming more and more difficult to negotiate.

When Oona's master opened the door he gave a start of astonishment.

"Why, why," he stammered, "I thought this was my cabin."

"I dare say it is," returned Mrs. Mount-Dyce-Mount. "I'm just staying in it for the time being."

"But, my God—don't you know we're going down?"

"Of course I do," she returned, irritably, "that's why I said for the time being."

"But you can't stay here! You'll drown! Don't you realise that? Where is your life preserver?"

"I couldn't get it on. I'm not the right shape. I just couldn't get it on. Then everybody was jostling so, I got my ankle turned and some young people almost knocked me over and I was frightened and I came in here. But — this dear little dog — I wish you could save him ! "

Oona's master took her by the arm and lifted her to her feet.

" You must come at once ! " he said, sternly.

The old lady clung to his shoulder and began to cry a little. He quickly opened a drawer and took out a packet he had come back for.

" Would you mind," he asked, " sending this to the address written on it — if you have the opportunity ? "

" Certainly, I shall," she answered, and put the packet into her handbag.

Tim paid no heed to these proceedings. He was occupied by Oona's sudden condescension towards him. She, who had never given him a glance, was now delicately sniffing him all over. Her strong tail was wagging approval of him. When she thrust her muzzle under his chest she lifted him off his feet. She uttered a low whine of pleasure in him.

The Captain and his officers had been able to quiet the hysterical passengers. The second last of the lifeboats was about to be lowered into a sun-gilded sea. A dozen hands reached out to help Mrs. Mount-Dyce-Mount.

The vessel was sinking fast. There was not a moment to spare. Oona's master picked up Tim and dropped him into the old lady's lap.

He perched on her knees, alert in every nerve. His restricted life of the past week had been opened up to an almost overpowering breadth. There was so much to see. All that was needed to make his exhilaration complete was cats !

Still he could see Jean and John clinging together in a boat quite near and he began to bark at them loudly, vindictively, with a kind of strangling snarl between each explosion. John called out :

" Mrs. Mount ! Throw that dog out ! He's mad ! It's not safe for you to hold him ! "

" Yes, he's quite mad ! " cried Jean. " He'll bite you ! "

Tiny Tim barked the louder and Mrs. Mount-Dyce-Mount held him close.

The last lifeboat was lowered. The Captain, some sailors, a stoker and Oona and her master were in it. He had refused to leave her and they found room for her in the boat. The waves were mounting higher, a sudden squall broke and the ship, shaken as though by a great convulsion, rolled over and sank. A driving storm of sleet and snow blurred the vision, so that the occupants of the lifeboats became isolated and felt small and weak and afraid.

All but Tim.

He stood tiny, shivering, indomitable, on Mrs. Mount-Dyce-Mount's lap. With his bright eyes he strove to pierce the blurring, icy flakes. His instinct was directed towards Oona and all his eager senses sought to search her out. When a bitter wave slashed across the lap where he was braced, he lifted a paw and stood shivering on three legs.

The squall passed and the sun rose ruddy and beautiful for Christmas morning. The ship had disappeared

and two of the lifeboats had been swamped. The
waves were romping with the wreckage and with the
bodies of those who clung to it.

Tim soon discovered John and Jean clinging
together in the sea, more dead than alive. He showed
his little teeth in rage at their nearness and gave out
such a volley of barks as almost threw him over-
board.

Then he saw Oona and his barking ceased. She
was swimming round and round as though searching
for something. Her grand rugged head looked
grander still, rising out of the foam. Tim strained
towards her trembling, uttering little plaintive
whimpers.

The SOS had been heard and another ship was
already coming to the rescue. The wind fell, the sun
rose and a feeble cheer was raised.

John and Jean were the first to be picked up. The Captain, the sailors, the stoker, all those who had been in that last lifeboat were saved — all but Oona and her master. And she might have been saved but, when they tried to reach her she swam out of their way, her gaunt head raised, her sombre eyes searching the waves.

JUSTICE FOR AN ARISTOCRAT

THERE was a group of men about a charcoal stove in the street outside the military barracks. The men were digging a drain and half-frozen earth lay in drab lumps in the roadside. Snow was beginning to fall and the air had that peculiar harsh greyness which takes the colour from the face and intensifies every line and blemish. The men's faded clothes, their lumpish shapes, their thick irregular features, seemed a mere gathering together and enlivening of the earth itself. Only the fiery glow of the charcoal gave a soul to the scene.

But the men were the reverse of depressed. They were strong in belief in the superiority of their position as compared with the labourers of other countries. They knew that the workers owned their country and that, at last, the workers had justice and administered justice. They were free. They were strong. It was not like the old Czarist days of injustice and oppression.

" It's terrible to think," said Ivan Popoff, unwrapping his packet of half-frozen bread and taking an enormous bite, " how other countries are still under the heel of capitalists and tyrants."

" The workers of Russia own everything," said Peter Rakatin, his words struggling to utterance against a chunk of gristle.

Mitya Grushinka, a gaunt, curly headed boy, stared into their mouths enviously. His scrap of food had been swallowed up in a moment. " Just the same," he said, " there must have been some pretty sights in the old days. I am too young to remember."

" Pretty sights won't fill your belly," returned Peter, champing the gristle. " The workers of Russia own everything."

" I know we do," said Mitya. " My father has told me how, in the old days, the sleighs of the nobility used to go gliding over the snow, with fur rugs hanging from the back and silver bells jingling. Once, my father says, a lady dropped her muff out of the sleigh and he picked it up and ran after and returned it to her. The gentleman gave him a silver piece and the lady, who was very beautiful, waved her muff and laughed."

" Well, it's our turn to laugh now," said Ivan grimly.

Peter shifted the gristle to the other side of his mouth. " The workers own everything," he said.

" My mother," went on Mitya, spreading his thin young hands to the heat of the charcoal, " says that the processions on Holy days were beautiful. They made you forget all your worries."

63

"Religious ceremonies! Drugs! Drugs! Drugs
— to make you forget!" said Ivan. "We have
sent God packing. We have no more use for
God."

"We don't acknowledge that he made the world,"
said Peter. "We made it ourselves. We made our
own world. It's ours."

"My grandfather," said Mitya, "still keeps an
ikon in a corner of the room. He burns a bit of
candle in front of it. It looks pretty in the corner
when one goes home cold and tired."

"Pretty be damned!" said Ivan. "Your grandfather ought to be ashamed of himself. But then he
is an old fool."

"He knows that. But he says he's too old now
to give up God. He's got so used to God that he
wouldn't know how to get on without him."

Peter bolted the gristle. "I get on without God,
and look at me!"

"You look just like a frog," said Mitya.

They were ready to quarrel when their attention
was caught by a man coming along the road leading
a horse. On either side of the horse walked a soldier
with his bayonet over his shoulder. Motor cars and
lorries moved aside to make way for them and people
walking on the pavement stopped to stare in curiosity
at the beautiful beast.

His approach, through the mechanical drabness of
the traffic, seemed the approach of a conqueror. He
lifted his hoofs and put them down again with the
precision of a musician's fingers on the keyboard.

64

There was majesty in the moving lines of his superb body, and the elegance of his raised head annihilated the pretensions of what moved about him. He wore no saddle, but his bridle was held in the hand of a groom whose face wore the stamp of grief.

The group stopped outside the Court-house and at once the gate of the yard was thrown open by a porter who called out :

" This way with the prisoner ! "

The porter was fully conscious of the effect of his words on the men about the charcoal fire and on the loiterers that were already gathering about the gate. He showed his yellow teeth proudly under his enormous moustache and gave a mock ceremonious bow to the horse.

Led by the groom, guarded by the soldiers, he passed through the gate and it was shut with a frozen clang behind him. But the porter remained on the outside and stood, his back against the gate, waiting for questions.

They came fast enough. What was taking place ? Who owned the horse ? Was the Court turning into a circus ? Was the judge going for a ride ? Mitya was the only one who did not ask questions. He stood, with his eyes fixed blankly on the closed gate, as though his soul had mounted the horse and passed through with it.

" It is a court-martial," answered the porter, mouthing the words in zest under his frozen moustache. " It is as true a court-martial as ever you saw. All the ceremony is there — the officers in full

65

uniform, but — it is held out-doors, for the benefit of the prisoner who is not accustomed to rooms and their furniture."

" But who is the prisoner ? " asked Ivan.

" He is the horse you saw."

" The horse ! " cried Mitya. " But what can he have done ? "

" In the first place he is an aristocrat. The son of a famous sire, Sunstar. That is bad enough."

" It is certainly bad," said Peter. " He should be put to work — made to draw a dung cart."

" No. He is to be given a fair trial, with witnesses for and against. If he is found innocent of the crime he will be set free."

" But how can a horse commit a crime ? " asked a woman with a child in her arms.

" I will tell you. This horse won a silver cup at the Royal Horse Show. And who offered this cup ? Who offered it ? " He glared into the faces about him.

No one knew.

" Then I will tell you. It was the late Czar ! He offered the cup and this horse, Moonstar, won it ! If you want my opinion, I will tell you that I don't think that he has the ghost of a chance of acquittal." He looked about him proudly.

After a little the group by the gate scattered, the labourers returned to their work. Mitya could think of nothing but the beautiful horse, the way he had lifted his feet, as though he knew the beauty of his every movement, the way he raised his head, as though a wind were in his face, the glance of gentle pride he had cast at the porter when he threw open the gate. Above the sound of the picks in frozen earth Mitya listened for the sound of horse's hoofs.

At last they sounded on the pavement of the court-yard, rhythmic as music, drawing nearer with every beat. The porter threw open the gate with a flourish, as though he had himself created a tableau, and there again stood the horse, the groom and the armed soldiers on either side. But now there were six soldiers instead of two.

" Found guilty ? " questioned the porter.

" Found guilty," answered the groom, his mouth twisted in pain. He led the horse into the road.

The gate clanged shut. The soldiers marked time on the freezing ground. " Right wheel ! " shouted the one in command. " March ! "

Mitya threw down his spade. " I'm going after them," he said. " I want to hear more about the horse."

" You can't do that ! " cried Ivan. " You'll lose your job."

But the boy did not care. He followed the horse through the streets, marching in step with the soldiers till they turned into a row of stables belonging to the army. But, when Mitya would have followed, a soldier barred his way.

" You can't come in here," he said.

" But I want to touch the horse."

" Is the fellow a fool ? " asked another soldier, coming up.

" No, I'm not a fool," answered Mitya for himself.

" It is only that I've never seen such a beast before and I'd like to stroke him."

The new Bolshevic Army had not a strict discipline. Mitya was allowed to follow the horse and groom into the stable.

He stood there astonished, staring at the rows of rounded, muscular flanks projecting from the series of stalls. He was used to motors of all sorts but he had never given a thought to horses. Their primitive power, their strange beauty gave him a feeling of sadness, as for something unattainable.

The groom had led the condemned horse into a loose-box and was taking off the bridle. Mitya could see that he was crying.

" Do you think it was a fair trial ? " he asked.

" Be careful," answered the groom, " that no one hears you. Yes, I suppose it was a fair trial, though the poor creature couldn't know he was doing wrong."

" Can I come in and stroke him ? "

The groom nodded and Mitya went into the loose-box. The smell of clean straw rose to his nostrils, the smell of polished leather and a strange sweet animal smell from the horse. Free of his bridle he flung up his stark head, the whites of his eyes showing above the lustrous iris, the rosy nostrils spread as though to drink in the very fountain of life. He danced sideways from Mitya, as elegantly as a tight-rope walker, then bent his head, bowing until his mane fell into his eyes.

" He's full of fun," said the groom. " He doesn't realise how things are with him."

" What are they going to do to him ? "

" Shoot him. To-morrow morning."

" Oh. . . . Do you think he'd let me stroke him ? "

" If I say. He does what I tell him. You've no idea how glad he is to be alone with me again. He didn't like that trial, I can tell you. There they stood in their uniforms, looking solemn — talking, talking, and everything strange to him. When the sentence was pronounced he reared and lifted his fore-hoof, as though to strike, but it was just because he was angry at standing there so long."

" Perhaps he didn't like the looks of them."

" Perhaps not. They laughed and one said, — ' Well, at this time to-morrow, you'll be only horse meat ! ' "

" Will you tell him to let me stroke him ? "

" Quiet, Moonstar, quiet, my pet ! This young boy won't harm you."

The horse stood gentle while Mitya passed his hands over his sides which were the colour of a newly split chestnut, and his neck that had the lovely curve of a harp.

" How firm he is ! You'd think he was a different kind of flesh."

" I shouldn't mind if they shot me with him to-morrow."

" Well, I don't understand. What was he for ? What use was he ? "

" God help us ! Did you never see a gentleman riding ? Did you never hear of a horse show ? I wish you might have seen his owner mounted on him. He was as fine a man as this is horse."

Mitya ran his fingers through the strong silk of the mane. " Is the owner dead, then ? "

" Yes. They shot *him* six months ago. I've cared for the horse ever since. I never thought they'd be after him."

" It's a good thing he doesn't understand, isn't it ? "

" I shall bandage his eyes, so he won't see the muskets raised. . . . Why, when I look at him standing here I can't believe in it all. If he chose he could jump over their heads as if they were rats. You ought to see him jump. He gathers himself together like a cloud. He looks at the barrier. He clears it like lightning — then skims on to the next one. He shows himself off like a prince. Ay ! That's the trouble ! Like a prince ! "

" Might I have a few hairs of his mane to keep ? " asked Mitya.

" Yes ! Yes ! I'll give you a lock of his mane. I'm glad you thought of that. I'll cut a lock for myself, too."

The horse stared, with a kind of glowing wonder in his eyes, as with a pair of clippers the groom cut a thick lock from the richness of his mane and divided it between Mitya and himself.

All the rest of the day Mitya was conscious of the lock of hair in his pocket. Now and again he would put in his fingers to make sure it was there. When evening came he sat in a corner of the room with his grandfather and told him about the horse. The candle before the ikon cast a glow on their faces, making each in his way beautiful.

Mitya was early at work. He kept looking down the road for the approach of the horse. It was very cold and red sunlight flamed on the window panes of the barracks when at last he saw him coming.

" Here he is ! " he cried and he straightened himself and ceased digging.

" Who ? " demanded Ivan.

" Him — who's going to be shot."

" We workers own the country," said Peter, " and we must see that justice is done. He will make good meat, that beast."

" Don't ! " said Mitya, beginning to cry.

The hoof-beats sounded muffled, for there had been a light fall of snow. The groom walked in his best clothes, very upright but looking as though he had not slept. His mouth had sunk into his grey face in despair.

But the horse moved in the red sunlight as though he were a god of the sun. In purity of rhythm his muscular neck moved against the noble arch of his shoulders. His eyes beamed in proud confidence as he followed the groom.

The porter was there to throw open the gate. A second group of soldiers was waiting inside. At the end of the barrack yard Mitya had a glimpse of the firing squad. The three labourers leant on their spades listening.

The frosty air was shivered by an explosion, as though the fiery ball of the sun had burst.

" That's the end of him," said Ivan.

" As of all enemies of the State," said Peter.

Mitya began to dig wildly, throwing the earth about. He kept his eyes fixed in the hole he was digging and would not look as the sledge bearing the body of the horse passed through the gate.

APRIL DAY

A Sketch in Temperaments

IT was seven in the morning and the Scottie and the Cairn knew that soon it would be time to get up. They heard stirrings in the house below. They slept on the top floor in a dressing-room between the bedrooms of their mistresses, Zia and Cara. The two round dog baskets, with the cretonne cushions exactly alike, stood side by side. Dan, the Scottie, was able to look straight into Robbie's face.

Out of his almond-shaped eyes that were set high in his hard brindle head, Dan gazed lovingly into Robbie's face, veiled in fine grey hair which stood in tremulous half-curls on his brow, curved into a tiny moustache on his lip, and turned velvet and close on his ears.

April Day

Robbie knew that Dan was staring at him and the love did not matter, for, at this moment, he wanted nothing but to be let alone. He was savouring the last delicious doze before the moment when he would spring out of his basket. He kept his eyes shut tight. His head rested against the side of the basket helpless-looking, like a little child's.

Dan stared and stared. A quiver ran down his spine, making the tip of his tail vibrate. He was sixteen months old and Robbie had had his first birthday last week. Dan seemed much the older, for he often had a dour look. He poured out his soul in love to Robbie all day long.

Now a felt-slippered step shuffled outside the door and it opened a little way. The cook put in her head. " Come, boys, come now, time to get up," she said and held the door open wide enough for them to pass through.

Dan jumped from his basket and reared himself on his hind legs. He waved his fore-paws at the cook, but she had barely a word for him. Robbie was her charmer.

Now, as he coyly descended the stairs behind her, she encouraged him with endearments. At each landing he lay on his back and rolled, talking to himself in a low pleasant growl.

" Come along, darling, do," urged the cook, half-way down the stairs but she had to plod back to the landing to persuade him.

Dan had gone down the two flights of stairs like a bullet. Now he stood waiting by the open front door, looking back over his shoulder. When Robbie reached the bottom step, Dan ran out and Robbie after him.

They went to their usual place under the weeping rose tree that was newly in leaf. The sun had just risen above the great shoulder of the nearest hill. The spring morning lay spread before them, to the distant mountains of Wales.

Shoulder to shoulder they trotted round the house and up the slope, pushing aside the faces of daffodils and narcissus, hastening a little as they neared the denseness of trees. Among the trees there was a moist mossy twilight and across it flitted the brown hump of a young rabbit. Dan saw it first. He gave a cry, as of agony, and hurled himself into the wood. With a little moan of bewilderment Robbie flew after him, not yet knowing what he chased.

Head to tail, they dived into the green twilight. The rabbit whirled beneath the prickly fortress of a holly bush. Out at the other side it flew, skimming the wet grass, its ears flat in stark terror. Dan circled the holly bush, screaming.

Now Robbie was sure that what they were pursuing had escaped, though he had never known what it was. He stood pensive a moment, listening to Dan's screams, then drifted back toward the house. He found the front door shut, as the cook did against their return, so he went to the green knoll outside the kitchen window and sat there under the green-and-white spread of the sycamore tree. He looked imploringly, from under his fine fringe, into the window at the cook bending over the range, at the maid putting on her cap, tucking her curls beneath it.

He heard the clump of a step on the cobbled path and saw the milkman coming with his carrier of milk. It was a shock to find that he had drawn so near without molestation. Robbie hurled himself down the knoll, screaming and champing at the milkman's legs. The cook came out of the kitchen calling :

" Robbie ! Robbie ! He won't hurt you ! He's as gentle as a lamb ! "

She said this every morning to the milkman who never believed her but came on grumbling. The cook picked Robbie up and he let his head rest against her bosom. She still held him a moment after the milkman had gone. He was patient but he wanted to go upstairs.

As soon as she put him down he glided along the hall and up the two flights of stairs. He scratched on the door of the dressing-room. Zia opened it and she and Cara told him how good and beautiful he was. He lay on his back looking up at them gently but haughtily, savouring their homage. His pointed grey paws hung quiet.

He saw the gas fire burning and stretched himself before it.

At first Dan did not miss Robbie, then suddenly realised that he had gone back to the house. What might not Robbie be doing without him ? He tore across the grass, found the front door shut and barked insistently till it was opened by the maid.

On his short legs he pulled himself up the stairs

and scratched peremptorily on the door of the dressing-room. Inside he reared and walked on his hind legs for a few steps with the sturdy grace of a pony stallion. He rolled his eyes toward the cupboard where the big glass marble lived. Zia went to the cupboard.

" Oh, must he have that ? " said Cara. " It makes such a noise ! "

" He says he must," said Zia. She laid the glass marble, with the silver bear in its middle, on the floor.

With a growl of joy, Dan pounced on it. He struck it with his paw, then bounded after it. Up and down the room he chased it, pushing it swiftly with his nose then panting after it, banging it against the wall and, at last, between Robbie's paws.

Robbie hated the marble with a bitter hatred. The rolling and the noise of it made him feel sick. Now he lay, with half-closed eyes, guarding it between his paws. Dan looked up into Zia's face.

" Robbie's got my ball," his look said.

" Get it, then," said Zia.

Dan approached Robbie tremblingly, pretending he was afraid or really being afraid.

Zia gave him back the marble. He struck it with his muzzle, then flew after it growling. After a little he began to gnaw it.

" Enough ! " said Zia, taking it from him. " You'll ruin your teeth."

The four went down to breakfast. The dogs' plates stood waiting, filled with bits of hard-toasted brown bread. They crunched in delight, Dan's tail waving, Robbie's laid close. The moment they had finished they ran to the table to beg. Dan sat staring up out of glowing eyes. Cara dropped bits of bacon to him which he caught with a snap. Robbie mounted the arm of the settee behind Zia's chair. He put his paws on her shoulder and his cheek close to hers, so that she gave him bits of roll and honey.

At the first whiff of cigarette smoke Dan clambered into his basket and Robbie established himself on the fender stool, with his back turned to the table. He wore a look of disdain.

The children came in on their way to school. The dogs suffered themselves to be caressed but they wanted to doze.

As the sun shone warmer they went to the drive and stretched themselves at ease, ready for what might happen. Each time an errand boy came through the gate they went after him, exploding in barks as they ran. Cara or Zia or the gardener called to them, apologised for them, petted them for coming when they were called. They felt fearless and proud and obedient, wagging their tails after each sortie.

After a while the cook brought bones to them. She chose the biggest, hardest bone for Dan and the one with the most juicy meat on it for Robbie. But it was Dan who looked up at her in an ecstasy of gratitude ; Robbie who took his haughtily, as though it were no more than he had expected. They settled down with the bones, eyeing each other distrustfully before they began to gnaw.

Dan gnawed his bone in long steady grinds, wearing it down with his strong teeth, exposing its granular interior, arching his muscular neck above it. Robbie ripped the red meat from his, gnawed at the end where the marrow was, grew tired and rose with the bone in his mouth, looking about for a place to bury it.

Dan saw this with dismay. To bury so soon! It could not be done! He darted at Robbie and tried to take the bone from him. Robbie lifted his lip in a defensive sneer. He growled in his throat. Dan returned to his own bone.

After a little while Robbie glided into the shrubbery and began to dig in the moist mossy earth. He buried the bone well, drawing the earth over it with paws and delicate nose. He came out of the shrubbery just as Cara came out of the house.

" Too much bone," she said, " you're having too much bone." She went toward Dan.

He wagged his tail at her to take the sting from his ferocious growl. " Don't touch my bone! " he shouted. " Don't touch my bone! "

" You'd growl at me! " cried Cara, and she made a dart for the bone.

He caught it up and romped away from her.

Zia came out of the house with collars and leads in one hand and a dog brush in the other.

" Walkee, walkee," she said as she came. " Walkee, walkee! "

Dan dropped his bone and ran to her. Robbie danced toward her. Jealously Dan shouldered him away, pulling him gently by the ear. He loved him but he did not want him making up to Zia.

She took Dan in her hands and laid him flat. She

80

began vigorously to brush him. He stretched himself at full length, giving himself to the brush in delight, kicking joyfully when it touched a sensitive spot. He showed his teeth in a grin of love and beamed up at Zia.

When Dan was brushed Zia stretched out her hand for Robbie, but he slid from under it like water. He looked at her coyly from over his shoulder. He kept always just out of reach, as she followed him on her knees across the grass.

" Walkee, walkee," she cooed. " Brushee, brushee ! "

He bowed politely and touched her hand with his nose but was gone before she could catch him.

" Very well," said Zia, " we'll go without you."

She and Cara went into the house, ignoring Robbie. When they came down with their coats and hats on he was sitting on the pink best chair. Zia caught him up, sat down with him on her lap and began to brush him. He could tolerate this. He sat resigned as she brushed his long delicate hair first up, then down, then in a swirl to follow the streamline of his spine. But when she put the harness and lead on him he stiffened himself and an icy aloofness came into his eyes. He looked as aloof as a carved unicorn on the top of a stone gateway. He was not Robbie at all.

But he was himself again as he and Dan trotted down the drive and through the gate shoulder to shoulder, their mistresses on the other end of the leads. They turned from the main road into a country road past the fields where the new lambs were being suckled and the glossy hunters were nibbling the grass, past the duck-pond. Robbie averted his eyes from the ducks with a bleak look as though he could not bear the sight of them but Dan, now off the lead, looked at them with beaming interest. He beamed up at Zia. " What about it ? " his eyes asked.

" Don't dare ! " said Zia.

On and on they walked, the great hills always rising before them, the primrose wreathes palely blooming on the banks. But hills and flowers meant nothing to the dogs. The thousand scents of road and ditch meant much. A rabbit had passed this way. A weasel had passed that. Only an hour ago the Hunt had crossed the road.

Dan never wearied of the pleasures of the road. He jogged jauntily on and on as though he would go for ever. From a front view, one saw first his pricked ears, with the tail appearing exactly between them, then the strong shoulders, the bent elbows and the round paws that padded one over the other as though he were climbing a ladder.

Now Robbie was bored. He wanted to go home. He drifted along the road like a resigned little old lady with her grey shawl draped about her. He looked neither to right nor left.

They took the short cut home through the lane where the holly berries still shone bright among the prickly leaves. They found the break in the hedge. Zia lifted Dan over first, then followed him. Cara handed Robbie over and came last. She took off his harness and lead.

April Day

He stood crouching while it was undone, then sped forward like a slim grey arrow, past the house, past the stables, into the wildwood. Each breath was a protest against restraint. He felt free and cruel as a fox.

Now he was chasing a rabbit, all his boredom gone. Through the green twilight of the wood they sped, terror in one, joy in the other. Under the thick clammy leaves of rhododendrons, under the prickling boughs of holly, through thorny undergrowth that tore out locks of Robbie's hair and scratched his face. Neither he nor the rabbit uttered a sound. They flew silently, as though in a dream.

Then suddenly the rabbit was gone, swallowed up in a burrow. Robbie lay panting, his heart throbbing. He pulled some of the burrs from his paws and his tail. After a while he remembered his dinner, his home. He trotted along a path and was passing the orchard when he saw that the hens had been let out of their run and were strutting about among the daffodils.

He hesitated by a hole in the hedge and peered through at them. His eyes were bleak, as when he had turned his gaze away from the ducks. But now he did not turn away. He stared and stared. He was alone. There was no one to stop him.

He glided through the hedge and sprang fiercely on the nearest hen. She flapped her big red wings and ran squawking, with him on her back. She fell and still holding her by the neck, he threw her from side to side till she stopped struggling. All the other hens and the cock were in a panic, running here and there among the trees, each thinking it was its turn next. Robbie, with the face of a little gargoyle, ran after them. He whimpered in his delight.

The red feathers were scattered over the grass. Five bundles of them lay still and two more huddled in weakness and fear. The rest of the flock were safe in their run. Robbie stood looking in at them. They were all right there. That was where they belonged. In the orchard they were wild things to be pursued.

The front door stood open. He glided into the sitting-room. Dan was curled up in his basket, asleep after a good dinner, but he jumped out and came to meet Robbie. He sniffed Robbie's mouth and his tail quivered in recognition of the scent there. He grinned joyfully at Robbie.

But Robbie wanted his dinner. He went to the kitchen and found the maid. He danced about her, gently nipped her ankles in their black cotton stockings. She snatched him up and rocked him in her arms.

" Oh, baby, baby, little baby ! "

His beautiful eyes pleaded but she could not bear to put him down. She snuggled her rosy cheek against him, then held him at arms' length in her hands, adoring him. He looked at her, docile yet roguish. When she put her face near enough he gave her nose a swift nip. She hugged him close.

At last his plate was set in front of him, boiled cod mixed with vegetables. He ate less daintily than usual, for he was very hungry. Dan stood watching him and, when he had finished, came to his plate and licked it thoroughly. Robbie took a big drink out of the brown earthen dish, then went back to the sitting-room and stretched himself at length on the settee. Dan returned to his basket.

For some reason the settee did not satisfy Robbie, though generally it was his favourite spot. He jumped down and came to the basket and gazed in at Dan. Dan turned up his belly and rolled his eyes at Robbie but, after a little, he scrambled out of the basket and on to the settee. Robbie drifted into the basket.

While they were still drowsy Zia came with brush and comb and began to groom them. They were to go to the photographers and already they were late for the appointment but they must look their best. The car was at the door and now Zia slid under the wheel and Cara sat in the seat behind with a little dog on either side of her. They were as pretty as pictures, she told them.

They sat looking noble, till the car went into low gear on the steep hill and they felt the threat of the engine's vibration. They yawned and drooped, then hid their faces in Cara's lap and gave themselves up to misery. But on the level their spirits returned and they began to romp in exhilaration, growl at each other, stand upright on the seat, breast to breast.

What grand puppies, the photographer said, and placed them side by side on a settee and hid his head in the camera. That was only the beginning.

Dan jumped to the floor and, when he was lifted to the settee, Robbie jumped down. They did this till they were excited and panting and spoken to severely. Then they cowered on the settee, looking like curs. The photographer barked loudly and they had hysterics. Robbie suffered the photographer to put him on the settee and admonish him but Dan raised his voice and barked : " Don't touch me, man ! " He showed his teeth in a threatening grin. Then suddenly he was well behaved and posed nobly, sometimes in profile, sometimes full-face but always fine, like the prize-winner at a dog show.

Now there was only Robbie to cope with, but Robbie had become all wriggles and gaiety. Being photographed was funnier than he could bear. He lay on his back and kicked his joy in it.

Then, at last, he sat still. But now Dan was tired. He curled himself into a tight ball and fell asleep.

When he was raised he had no backbone but lolled and looked imbecile. Zia produced toffee and fed them. The trick was done! The camera clicked.

Now there was shopping and they sat alone in the car while Zia and Cara went into the shops. It was lonely in the car. Dan attended to his paws, licking them till his nails shone like ebony. Sometimes, by mistake, licking the cushion of the car. Robbie never licked his paws. He ignored sore spots which Dan would have licked incessantly. So, to pass the time,

Robbie gnawed the polished wood of the window frame. It was awkward to get at but he managed it. They were nearly home when Cara discovered the tooth-marks. " Which of you did this ? " she demanded sternly.

Dan looked guilty, contrite, but Robbie knew nothing about it. His eyes spoke innocence from under his silken fringe. Cara smacked the top of Dan's lean flat skull. He burrowed into a corner, ashamed.

Presently Robbie's thoughts returned to the window frame and he gave it a last gnaw as they passed through the gate.

" So — it was you, Robbie ! " cried Cara. " Oh, poor Dan, why were you so silly ? " She pulled Dan from his corner and patted him. Robbie leaped lightly from the car when it stopped and, pursued by Dan, sped into the wilderness. Soon they were chasing a rabbit and Dan's screams echoed among the trees.

They came back in time for tea. They stood shoulder to shoulder, yearning toward the teapot. They had their saucers of weak tea, then got into the basket together and slept.

The gardener stood, strong and bent, in the corner of the room, the loam scraped from his boots, his hands washed clean.

" Thur's been fowls killed," he said, " seven on 'em. Some time this marnin', it were. I think one o' our little fellers done it."

Cara turned pale. " How awful ! Are you sure it was one of ours ? "

" Thur's been no other on t' place, ma'am. T' gates is all shut fast."

He bent over the basket and with his gentle thick hand lifted Dan's lip and looked at the double row of white teeth laid evenly together, a little underhung but not much.

" Nubbut thure."

As gently but less cautiously he looked in Robbie's mouth. Quickly he folded down the soft lip. " 'Tis him, for sartin," he said quietly. " Thure's a bit o' feather between his teeth. I'm not surprised, ma'am. He killed one once afore. I caught him at it. He thinks they didn't orter be runnin' in t' orchard. But

'tis only a puppy. Don't you fret. He'll not do it again."

Robbie looked coyly up at them. He laid a pointed paw on each side of his face and looked up lovingly into Cara's eyes.

" He'll never do it again," comforted the gardener.

As the sun slanted in at the west window and the children were getting ready for bed, Dan and Robbie went to the nursery for their evening play. Dan romped with the children. He was rough with them, but they must not pull him about. " Have a care how you handle me ! " his warning growl came.

Robbie drifted about, always just outside the game. But, when the children caught him, he surrendered himself to be held uncomfortably in small arms, to be dandled on small hard knees.

Toward evening the air had become warmer. Without question the birds and flowers opened their hearts to summer. Starlings walked about the lawn, staring into daisy faces. Dan and Robbie lay before the door serenely facing the great spread of hills unrolled before them. Their sensitive nostrils put aside the smell of the wallflower and drank in what rich animal scents came their way.

They lay as still as carven dogs except for the faint fluttering of the hair on Robbie's crown. Dan faced the breeze with head stark, neck arched and thick like a little stallion.

When two gipsy women clumped up the drive selling mimosa the dogs did not bark but watched their coming and their going tranquilly. They were steeped in the new sweet warmth of the evening.

But when they were turned out for a last run before bedtime, it was different. The air came sharply from the highest hill. The earth sent its quickness up into them. Robbie ran into the wildwood but Dan found a hedgehog and worked himself into a rage before its prickles. Cara and Zia found him in the blackness beneath a yew tree and turned the beam of an electric torch on him. On the bright green of the grass the hedgehog sat like a bundle of autumn leaves, impervious.

" Open up ! Open up ! " shouted Dan, his teeth wet and gleaming.

Robbie came drifting out of the shrubbery and sat down watching the pair, knowing the hopelessness of the onslaught. Dan put his nose against the prickles and started back, shouting still louder : " Open up ! Open up ! "

But the hedgehog held itself close, impervious as a burr.

" Enough ! " said Zia and tucked Dan under her arm.

Cara pounced on Robbie. The hedgehog was left to his dreams.

Snug in their baskets they lay in the dressing-room, the velvet darkness pressing closer and closer. Dan lay stretched as though running but Robbie's four feet lay bunched close together. His head was thrown back, his ears tilted alert for the whispering of dreams. What did he hear ? The cry of a rabbit in a trap ? Or some ghostly cackle from the poultry-yard ?

He woke. He sat up in his basket and uttered a loud accusing bark at what had disturbed him. His own voice was comforting. He had never before barked so sonorously, so much like Dan. The comfort of the barking gave him deep peace. He kept on and on. Cara came in at the door. She turned on the light.

Robbie looked at her wonderingly, his little head pillowed on his pointed paw. Dan gave a sheepish grin and hung his head. He had got out of his basket to meet her.

" Naughty, naughty, naughty ! " said Cara. " Back to your bed, Dan ! Not another bark out of you ! "

Dan slunk back to his basket, curled himself close. . . .

The shadows would not let Robbie be. Out of them came mysterious things to disturb him. He went to the open window and sat on the ledge, framed in ivy. He barked steadily on an even more sonorous note. He had lovely sensations. He felt that he could go on till dawn.

But he heard the door of Cara's room open and, in one graceful leap, he was back in his basket. Small and stern, Cara entered the room. In her room Zia was lying with the blankets over her head. In shame Dan went to meet Cara.

" It is the end, Dan," she said mournfully. " You must go into the box-room by yourself."

She took his basket and he humbly followed her, stopping only to nozzle Robbie as he passed. She put him in the farthest, darkest corner of the box-room where, if he did bark, he would scarcely be heard. She went back to bed. There was beautiful quiet. Zia uncovered her head.

Robbie was alone now and he gave full vent to the trouble that was in him. He forgot all but the mournful majesty of his barking as he sat on the window ledge.

When Cara came into the room he disregarded her till she took him into her arms. Then he laid his head confidingly on her shoulder and gave himself up to what might befall. It befell that he was laid on the foot of her bed. It seemed almost too good to be true. Everywhere there was peace and slumber.

At half-past seven the cook heavily mounted the stairs. She opened the door of the dressing-room and saw the one empty basket. She knocked on Cara's door and opened it.

" Half-past seven, madam," she said, " and I can't find the puppies at all ! "

" Dan is in the box-room. Robbie is here."

Dan and Robbie met in the passage. They kissed, then pranced about each other joyfully. They nipped the cook's ankles as they descended the stairs. Another April day had begun !

THE SHE GULL

THE downs above the sea were a lovely green after
the late rains. The sun divided his splendour
equally between land and water — resting on the one,
moving in countless swift gleams on the other. I
had found a hollow, sheltered by a thorn-bush, where
I had eaten my sandwiches and then smoked a cigarette, meditating on the fact that my holidays were
nearly over, that this would probably be my last

walk by the sea that year. I looked at my hand that had turned, since my arrival, from a pasty white to a rich coffee colour. I felt in my body the strength these downs, this sea had given me.

I lay staring straight ahead at the clear stretches of green and blue, unaware of the indigo cloud that was rising behind me, till it threw a foreboding shadow and the thorn-bush was shaken by a sudden gust. The cloud, fan-shaped, spread threateningly against the clear sky. It seemed moved by an active, conscious power, engendering darkness and fear. From its depths came a deep roll of thunder. I collected my book and my stick and began to walk swiftly toward the nearest houses — a fishing hamlet that was hidden between two cliffs. The gust had passed but was succeeded by a squally wind that took away my breath as I climbed the bare and grassy steep.

The wind appeared to come from the very heart of the cloud which, still keeping its fan shape, spread lower and darkened all the land. The sea lay brilliant in sunlight but with a strange, chill crispness. A flock of gulls that had been walking about a sunny slope, like geese grazing on a pasture, now rose and began to swoop and circle on the wind with loud cries. They moved, as it seemed, in an intricate design, of the pattern of which they were masters. Now in the black shadow of the cloud, now in the glittering air above the sea, they beat their strong wings or sailed effortless, unruffled as sculptured birds.

In watching them I almost forgot the approaching storm. In truth, I felt something of their wild pleasure in it. But soon a tremendous clap of thunder brought me to myself. Great raindrops struck my face as I strove against the now fierce wind. I saw that I was to be caught in the worst of the storm long before I reached the shelter of the village.

Then, beyond me, rising on the next promontory, I saw the coastguard's little house, white and trim, friendly as a beacon in darkness. It was, in fact, almost dark when I reached the door. The cloud, shapeless now, spread over land and sea. Under its brooding immensity there lay the purple tones of funeral plumes. The gulls still sailed and swooped above me. I had the thought that they had followed me, either in detached amusement at my puny battling against the gale, or in malicious hope that I might be driven over the edge of the cliff. The thunder was deafening as I knocked on the door but the coastguard heard me and opened it at once. Hailstones were beating on us both before he had closed it behind me.

He seemed pleased by my arrival, beaming at me out of his sea-blue eyes and offering me his chair. But I preferred to stand and stare out at the storm now that I was safe from it. He looked on it with tolerance as little more than a squall. I should see, he said, what that coast could do in December, with the waves clamouring to tear down the cliffs, and the wind— well, he had many a time been forced to climb the steep to his house on hands and knees, and he and the guard who took shifts with him had each to shout to make the other hear above the din.

The She Gull

He was very snug in there, with his stove for making tea, his bunk and comfortable chair. He was a comfortable-looking person, with a ruddy face and a full grey beard. He told me that he had spent part of his life in Ireland. That accounted for the curious mixture of Devon accent and Irish brogue in his talk. He had nothing but good to say of the Irish. They had treated him well. One night he had fallen off his bicycle into a pond and some country people, hearing his cries, had run to his assistance. They had pulled him out of the pond just as though he had not been English. It annoyed him to hear things said against them. If you treated them right, they treated you right. "There beant anny finer folk in the wor-r-ld," he said.

As the cloud dispersed he let me look through his telescope into the troubled distance. I could see the lighthouse on Portland Bill. What interested me more was to watch the movements of the gulls which had disappeared in the squall and now rose above the edge of the cliff, startlingly white against the purple sky. They were like heavenly creatures.

"I suppose," I said, "that you know a good deal about their habits?"

He took his beard in his thick brown hand and turned to look out of the window. He spoke in rather a gruff tone. "Yes. I know a good deal about them. I've watched them close for years."

"Do you come to know one from the other?"

Without looking round, he answered: "There's some I couldn't mistake. There's good and bad among 'em — like us."

I tried to get him to talk more about them but he became taciturn. The sun was flickering out. I was about to go, when I remembered something, with a pang of compassion.

"Wasn't it near here," I asked, "that a young woman flung herself over the cliff last week?"

He turned to face me and his hand moved from his beard to his mouth. He pulled nervously at his lip.

"Aye," he said, "it was. She threw herself over out yonder, poor gur-r-l. I did not see her do it but I was one of them that gathered her up."

"An awful thing."

"It was. A man was lying out there, on the cliff's edge and he saw her come running. She ran straight over the edge. It was turrible to see her, he said. He's been bad ever since."

"Do you know what the reason was for her doing such a thing?"

"Jealousy. That's what it was. The same old reason. She'd been walking out with Jarge Hayball for two years. We all wondered what such a fine gur-r-l saw in him, but there it was, she loved him passionate. I reckon she was almost too much for him. He took to meeting a pretty waitress from one of the hotels, on the sly. She was bound to find it out. They had a turrible scene. Folk said they saw her mourning on the road, wringing her two hands, then raising up her arms to heaven like wings, while he stood, with his face twisted like a dish-clout, not knowing what to say for himself."

The gulls swept past the windows like a white

banner, fluttered for an instant. The sun shone strongly on their broad wings. The guard looked after them as though absorbed in their movements. Though I spoke to him again he did not answer. I felt that the subject of the girl's suicide was a painful one which I should not have opened.

As it turned out, I came back to this same fishing village for my Christmas holidays. There was something in the place that fascinated me. I came back to it almost against my will, for I knew that it would likely be stormy and bleak there. Still, it was not the sort of place where Londoners go to spend a " country Christmas." I would have my boarding-place to myself — one great attraction. I arrived on the morning of Christmas and, as I had expected, I found wild weather and a blustering sea. The waves rushed as though in mad joy one after the other against the cliffs. They seemed not discouraged by their failure to drag it down with them but slid back foaming for renewed attack.

In the afternoon I thought I would walk to the coastguard's house. The sun was shining when I set out but, as on the day of my first meeting with him, a great cloud appeared from beyond the downs, not fan-shaped this time but a dark curtain, heavy with snow. I had to bow myself against the wind as I climbed the steep toward the stern little house that faced it so uncompromisingly. Through the window I saw the head of the guard silhouetted against the sky. His grey beard was grasped in one hand and he was motionless as the brow of the cliff.

I was hesitating as to whether or not I should disturb him when he turned suddenly and saw me. He gave a sharp start, as though alarmed, then recognised me and came at once to the door. He appeared glad to see me beyond the measure of our acquaintance. Whatever his thoughts had been he was willing enough to part with them. He seemed surprised when I told him that I had returned of my own accord to spend Christmas by the sea.

" 'Tis a queer, lonely time here," was his comment.

" But I like it," I insisted. " I prefer the company of gulls any day to that of most people."

He gave a sudden sardonic laugh. " Well," he said, " I can tell 'ee I don't ! I knows too much about 'em. The quarest critters in the wurrld, they be." As he spoke he started from the window and a large full-breasted gull hung before the pane for a space and looked squarely in at us, the bright eyes in the snow-white face giving it a look of almost angelic purity, yet set in such a way that more than a hint of malice was suggested.

As the bird sank below the level of the sill, I said : " He's a fine-looking fellow."

" Fellow ! " repeated the guard. " Not much ! It's a she ! It's *her* ! "

" *Her ?* " I repeated, bewildered.

" And why not ? " he exclaimed, almost testily. " Have you never heard tell of human souls going into animals and birds after death ? "

" I have," I returned doubtfully. " Yet you are not one of the people I should have expected to

believe in any such " — I held back the word " super-
stition," which I saw he was watching for and added
— " transformation."

" Call it what you like," he said. " I believe in it
because I've seen it and I know it's true. As true as
that God made this wurrld and put quare critters
into it."

I looked at him with some compassion. I felt that
the loneliness of his life was telling on his nerves. I
said : " I'm afraid I don't know who you mean
when you say *her*."

He moved restlessly across the cramped space of
the floor then spread his hands above the stove
though the room was hot. " I suppose I shouldn't go
talking about it," he said, " putting ideas into other
folk's heads. But I can't help it ! I've never told a
living soul till to-day and I'd not tell you if you
wasn't a stranger and going away in a day or so."
He fixed his eyes full on my face and said with great
solemnity : " The gull you saw looking in at us just
now was *her* — the gurrl that flung herself over the
cliff last summer ! "

Perhaps it was the strange isolation of our position,
the thunder of the sea against the cliffs, the snow that
began to fall like a mysterious veil about us. Whatever
it was I felt no great surprise at what he said, no
incredulity made my face unresponsive. He looked
in it eagerly. He went on :

" It was scarcely three days after she threw herself
over that I began to notice this gull. It was somehow
different from the rest. It acted strange-like and

though it was big and strong it didn't seem to know just how to use its wings. It would walk along the top of the cliff, just in front here, looking back at the land as though it was longing for something. I couldn't get the sense o't. The other gulls knowed it was strange. But they liked it. They flew and swooped about it, crying out and screeching but not angry. They brought it fish and fed it and before long it was as strong and swift and fierce as any of them. But it always liked the land and every now and again it walked along the path that leads towards the village and peered down it as though expecting someone. The thought came to me sudden that it was the spirit of the gurrl and I've never changed my mind. I'm surer of it every day. I see things that make me certain."

I perceived with anxiety that the hand he held over the stove was trembling. I told him that I had been chilled by the walk up the cliff and asked him if he had a drop of brandy he could give me. He got some from a cupboard and at my suggestion took a swallow or two himself. He walked to the window and looked out. Suddenly he took me by the sleeve and drew me towards it.

" There she is ! " he said pointing. " She's waiting for him. And he'll come ! He'll not fail her ! He dursn't ! She's got him where she wants him. In a cleft stick. His day's work'll be done now and he'll be coming up the cliff to meet her."

I looked out at the bird which strutted leisurely across the face of the cliff, looking now this way now that and immaculately white as the snowflakes which fell about her. I shivered and drew away from the guard's hand.

" There he comes ! " he almost shouted. " Don't you see him ? Just his head and shoulders ! He's having a time to climb the path against this wind." He stared in fearful fascination at the approaching figure which I could barely make out. I said, though I did not believe my own words : " I expect it is the other guard."

" He's not due for nearly an hour. No — this is Jarge Hayball. Make no mistake about that. My God ! Just see her a-going down to meet him ! "

The gull was indeed advancing toward the man who laboured against the wind up the steep slope. She showed unmistakable pleasure in his coming, swelling out her breast, trailing her wings and cocking her head first on this side, then on that. As he reached her she flew heavily to his shoulder and peered into his pallid face. Her wing knocked off his hat and it was instantly blown over the cliff but he took no notice of this. His head, crowned by thin curling hair, turned towards her in terrible fascination while she clung amorously to his sloping shoulder.

" Just see her ! " exclaimed the guard, hoarsely. " That's what I have to look at every few nights ! "

" Poor devil ! " I said.

" Well, he caused her death, didn't he ? 'Tis said she was going to have a child. I thought so myself, when I took up the body."

It was strange, it was horrible, yet — I felt pity

for the wretch who was impelled to this fantastic rendezvous. As he turned his face to the gull's she became coy and looked over her shoulder, out toward the sea. Then suddenly, with a quick movement of her pliant neck, she turned back and placed her beak upon his lips. She must have given this caress fiercely for he drew back his head as though in pain and put up a hand to ward her off.

"I can't stand this!" I cried. "I'm going out to him!"

But the guard laid a restraining hand on my arm. "If I can bear to see her love-making time and again, surely it won't harm 'ee to view it once."

"Has the other guard seen nothing?"

"No, but he's bound to one of these days."

As we spoke the shadow darkened. The snow was driven in heavy flakes into the sea. I saw that the man in moving backward from the gull had stepped dangerously near to the edge of the cliff.

"Look out!" I shouted but of course he could not hear me. Suddenly the gull rose from his shoulder and hung before his face beating her great wings, striking his features with her beak. He threw up his arms to ward her off but he stepped still closer to the brink of the promontory. In another moment he would be over the edge.

The coastguard and I rushed out through the door. There was no hesitation now on his part. He shouted as he ran and waved his arms to affright the gull. Other gulls had risen from the shelter of the cliff and began to circle about, uttering strange wild cries.

The She Gull

The she-gull beat on the man's face with her wings and, frantic with fear, he now struck at her savagely. He saw us running to his help and cried out to us.

It was a strange and confused scene — the snowy dusk descending on the cliff, the crashing waves below, the white shapes of the flying gulls lacing in and out among the figures of us humans, the interlacing wings and arms of the two who strove on the brink. Then he was gone. He was over the edge — just before the guard and I reached him ! It seemed unbelievable. One instant he was there, surrounded by the white forms of gulls. The next he had disappeared — without a cry and where he had stood the great white gull hovered, uttering long-drawn, clear cries which I could only take for cries of triumph.

We ran to the edge of the cliff and looked down. The tide was in and the white-veiled breakers rushed up the beach in the stormy twilight. There was a clear drop of nearly three hundred feet. The gull drifted down the cliff side, leaning softly on the wind, till she touched the waves. Then she rode on her white bosom while the others, sweeping in her wake, fell like snowflakes on the sea.

When I left the place I felt that I should never want to see it again but, when summer came round, its attraction for me drew me once more to its wild cliffs. The shock to my nerves had been great but that was now past and I felt a strong desire to see the coastguard again and ask him if there had been any sequel to the tragedy.

How different everything looked on this, my third

visit, to the coastguard's house ! It shone with a fresh coat of paint, sky and sea were of that amazing blue with which the South coast sometimes challenges Italy. The vivid green turf was springy beneath my feet as I swung across the downs. A fishing-boat with a red sail moved lightly toward the harbour of the hamlet. A group of gulls followed it, swooping and crying for the fish with which it was laden. I found my friend the coastguard looking more cheerful than when I had last called on him. We talked of this and that while he waited for the question that was hovering on my lips. Presently it came :

" Have you seen anything of *her* lately ? "

" Oh, her's always about." He spoke laconically, but his lips were stretched in a grim smile. I wondered how he could smile with such a recollection in his mind. But he was a strange man and he lived a strange, lonely life here.

"Do you think there is a chance of my seeing her?" Looking at the summer scene beyond his window I could scarcely believe in the tragedy I had witnessed there.

" Why, yes. Anyhow, I can show you where she has nested." Again the smile flickered across his face.

" Nested ! " I repeated, on an incredulous note.

" Aye. Why not ? Her was always a fine gurrl. Her's reared two families this season."

He took my arm and led me to the small window at the side. He pointed to a jagged pinnacle of rock that rose high and slender out of the sea. " On the very top of that," he said, triumphantly. " Nothing else would do her. She'd have her young where naught could harm 'em. Look — there now she goes with her second brood ! "

The great gull swept by the window with her grey young ones about her. She was teaching them the mysteries of flying and swooping and sailing on the breeze. She was paying special attention to a smaller weaker one, flying close beside it and encouraging it with strong maternal cries.

I hardly dared put the next question. I looked the other way, shamefaced, as I asked : " Have you seen — has anything of the sort — happened to the young man ? "

The coastguard directed my gaze out of the middle window where, on a sunny patch of turf, stood as miserable a looking gull as I have ever seen.

" That's Jarge ! " he said, pointing a finger at him. " She's mated with him, o' course, but he don't like the life."

And as he spoke Jarge stood, with unkempt plumage, pessimistically watching the swift gyrations of his mate and her young.

THE PONY THAT WOULD NOT
BE RIDDEN

HE was cobby and round and well fed, he was kind and sweet-tempered and strong — but nobody wanted him ! He spent his days and his nights in a field where sheep were pastured, on the side of a hill.   Other hills rose one after another to the purple hills of Wales in a glorious panorama but Lord Ronald saw only his hill, the small black-faced sheep that grazed on its shaggy side and the benevolent hump of the hayrick from which he pulled whenever he chose a wisp of sweet-tasting hay.   He would stand with his stocky legs well-planted, a wisp of hay dangling from the side of his mouth and stare tranquilly at his own hill, his companions the sheep and the kindly hump of the rick. Only one thing was lacking to him and that was a pair of legs he used to know.

Between himself and these legs there had existed a fond intimacy. They had talked to him in a language he could understand though sometimes he had pretended not to. There had been hands too, thin young girl's hands, on whose smooth palms he had mumbled with his sensitive upper lip for sugar. The voice that belonged to these legs and hands had been high and clear. Sometimes a silky mane had mingled with his own.

He had no definite longing for these but the memory of them sometimes stirred in him, vaguely but deeply, though it was two years since they were lost to him. He had a grand appetite. It was this that Farmer Goslett resented. There he was, a useless animal, eating the good hay and oats that might have fattened the young bullocks. The pony was mischievous too. In the long idle days he was often up to tricks that made for trouble. More than once he had forced an opening in the hedge, through which the sheep scattered themselves along the road and were chased by dogs. Another time he got himself caught in some barbed wire and there was a vet's bill.

He was a nuisance and he was an expense and he was no earthly use. Goslett did not know what to do about him. He had come by him in this way.

A family from South Africa had taken the dower house on a near-by estate for a term of years. There had been several schoolboys in the family and a little girl of eight. She was a delicate little thing but full of life. She was eager for a pony of her own and gave her father no peace until he bought one for her. The parents had been anxious to find a thoroughly reliable pony and it had been Goslett himself who had put this little Lord Ronald in their way. He was a handsome pony with a kind of sturdy nobility in his lines and he was guaranteed not to misbehave. He never had. He and the little girl became a familiar sight on the roads, he rounded and sturdy, she ethereally thin, her lank dark hair clinging about her neck and shoulders. She had a long, pointed face, large, rather startled-looking blue eyes and a mouth always ready to widen in a broad smile that showed two rows of lovely little teeth.

She was almost always smiling when she rode. She looked as happy as a foal in a spring meadow but the servants in the house said that her governess found her a handful and that she sometimes had tantrums that upset the whole household. Perhaps she had them because her health wasn't good. Every now and again she had a bout of illness. The neighbourhood had so taken her delicacy for granted that everyone was shocked when one morning, after the family had lived four years in the dower house, the news came that she had died the night before.

For four years she had cantered and galloped across the fields and along the roads on her pony. She had grown from a little thing of eight to a long-legged child of twelve. There had been something about her that had caught the eye and held it. When she was gone people spoke tenderly of her and it was some time before she was forgotten.

Her parents could not endure the house. They left their sons in England and went back to South Africa. They were not missed nearly so much as their child was.

The father had given the pony to Goslett because he had wanted to make sure of a kind home for him. Goslett said that his own young daughter would be glad to have him for riding to school. He thought to himself that he might make good use of him for light work on the farm.

But the first time that Lord Ronald felt Mary Goslett's fat legs pressed to his sides he refused to move. She coaxed and petted him but he hated the feel of her fat hands on his neck. When she spoke to him in her strong Herefordshire accent he quivered with displeasure. Her father and the labourer who worked for him, shouted to her to give him a taste of the whip. Mary did but Lord Ronald stiffened himself against the blows and did not budge. Not with ears laid back and an expression of wilful mulishness but simply as though he could not bring himself to move.

Then they coaxed him with sugar and carrots, the two men pushed him from behind but nothing would induce him to move. They tried him again the next day and the next and the next but neither beatings nor all the tricks they heard of from the neighbours were of any use. He stood like the shapely statue of a pony, immutable as granite, impervious to pain or cajolery. Mary Goslett was bitterly disappointed. She had liked the idea of showing off before the other children at the parish school, riding back and forth on the pony. The village children jeered at her. " The pony won't have naught to do with you, Mary. Him's used to little lady ridin' him ! "

When Goslett put the pony between shafts it was just the same. He planted his feet on the ground and nothing could move him. In other ways he was perfectly docile, trotting back to his friends the sheep after each trial with a gentle beam in his eyes, whether his sides were ridged with welts or the sweetness of sugar lay on his tongue.

It became a joke among the neighbours that Goslett's pony felt itself so far above him that it refused to do his bidding. In spite of his usual good sense he began to resent what seemed the pony's feeling of superiority. He said to his wife :

" It's damned swank, and no mistake. I've a mind to lather him 'til he drops where he stands."

" No," she answered, " his heart is just chronic with longing for his young lady and he won't tolerate any other rider. It's a rare disappointment for our Mary but you mustn't beat him any more. Folk will only laugh at you."

Lord Ronald was not beaten again but Goslett now made up his mind to sell him. He took him to a horse fair at a distance where no one had heard of his stubbornness. He had groomed him until he shone. His mane and tail were bright with energy.

His large blue-brown eyes had a friendly beam in them. There was no other such handsome pony at the fair.

But it was the same old story. When the would-be purchaser mounted him Lord Ronald turned into a statue that nothing could bring to life until once more the saddle was empty. Then he turned his glowing eyes from face to face, his velvet nostrils quivered against the damp air, and his small hoof pawed eagerly, as though he would be off.

" What d'ye think I want ? " cried the would-be purchaser. " A hobby horse ? "

Goslett was deeply chagrined. He led Lord Ronald home with his heart full of resentment. He turned him into a field and ignored him for the rest of the summer.

But when autumn came he again tried to master the pony. He had no success and again he led him to fairs and advertised him for sale. Lord Ronald was becoming well known. It put the horse-dealers, farmers and hostlers in good humour just to see him.

" Hullo, Jack ! " they would call. " Give us a ride on hobby-horse ! " Or — " 'Ere comes the favourite ! What odds be you offering, Goslett ? "

Goslett got to hate the pony. He would have given him away but nobody wanted him.

Now, two years after Lord Ronald had come into his possession, a gipsy offered to buy him. He had been passing in his cart and had seen the pony standing shapely and alert gazing across the hills. He had got out of the cart and gone to the farm gate and

leant on it, chirruping and talking in his gipsy lingo
to the pony. He had made some enquiries about him,
learned how he would allow no one to ride him.
Now he stood with Goslett at his side, looking him
over. His slender dark hands moved over Lord
Ronald's muscular body like two brown monkeys
intent on mischief. His soft eyes looked up sideways
into Goslett's face.

"I'll buy him of you," he said and he offered a
sum so low that Goslett could have knocked him
down for his cheek. This pony, this handsome
Scottish pony with his powerful loins, his lovely
shoulders, his coat that was like polished steel, when
he was groomed, though now it was muddy and
burrs clung in his mane, to be sacrificed as a gift to a
sly gipsy.

"'Tis no use buying him," growled Goslett. "He'd
not go for ye. He'll go for no man."

"He'll go for me," said the gipsy.

Goslett turned his slow gaze on him. He said:

"I'll not have him treated cruel."

The gipsy showed his pointed teeth. "I know a
trick or two," he said. "But I'd not hurt him."

"You don't know him. Get on his back and
you'll see what I mean. He's stubborn to the bone.
No trick of yours would budge him. But I don't
want him hurt."

"You want to keep him for the rest of his days,
eating his head off, eh?"

The gipsy smiled impudently into Goslett's face.
Then he placed his hands on Lord Ronald's back and

sprang, light as a panther, mounting him. He laid his slim body along the arch of the pony's neck and whispered in his ear.

The effect was startling to Goslett. Lord Ronald rose, as though touched by some secret spring in his inmost being, and stood erect on his hind legs. He stood so more than straight that it seemed he must fall backward at the next moment. He and the gipsy were turned into an equestrian statue of granite, wild, stark, almost terrifying.

"By gum! You've done it!" muttered Goslett. "You've made him move!"

Slowly, like a trained horse, Lord Ronald lowered himself until once more he stood on his four legs. He was trembling and sweat had turned the colour of his hide from steel to iron.

"Now you've done so much, why don't ye make him go with ye?" demanded Goslett. "A lot of good he'll be to ye, standin' on his hind legs like a circus pony!"

The gipsy slid to the ground. "Time enough later on. But you see I can make him move. He knows he's met his master."

"Well," growled Goslett, sullenly, "I'll take your offer. And I say you're a queer pair and I wish you luck with each other."

The gipsy promised to come back in three days with the money. Other gipsies were coming then with their caravan and they would take Lord Ronald away.

Goslett would be glad to see the last of the pony

but he wished he might have got rid of him in some other fashion. He had disliked the way he had broken into a sweat and trembled when the gipsy was on his back. He felt that he had almost sooner put a bullet through him and bury him in the pasture than see him led off by the gipsy. Still — money was money and in these hard days he needed it all too badly.

He and the gipsy stood talking a moment in the trampled mud outside the gate before they went their different ways, the gipsy dark and slender, a neckerchief tied about his throat, driving off in his cart, the farmer fair and thickset, his sturdy calves encased in leather leggings, trudging off with his sheep dog following at his heels. Neither turned to look back at Lord Ronald.

He stood watching their departing figures his large eyes dilated, one hoof pawing nervously at the frosty grass, the hairs of his mane and tail seeming separately alive.

The road ran through the farm and the labourer was now crossing it carrying the noon-day feed for the poultry which were in the meadow next Lord Ronald's pasture. As the labourer crossed the road with his bucket he was met by a flock of white leghorns that surged about him like a wave. They chanted their joy in his coming and a group of turkeys came, trailing their dark feet and crying plaintively for their share. The ducks left their pond across the road and rocked after the farm-hand, all but two who slumbered with heads tucked under wings among the reeds at the edge of the pond.

Lord Ronald was usually fascinated by the feeding of the poultry, putting his nose over the hedge and whickering to the man to make haste with the meal for himself and the sheep. But now he stood unmoved by the clatter of the hens or by the oncoming sheep that bundled themselves down the hillside toward the hayrick like a wind-blown patch of fog. Every now and again a tremor of fear shook him.

At last the man came and put down meal for him and for the sheep. The behinds of all the flock were turned to Lord Ronald. Their little black legs were rigid under their grey bodies, their black faces thrust into the meal. The man called.

" Coom along then, pony ! S'all I give yer feed to the sheep ? "

But he would not go.

All day the fog cloaked the countryside. The hills might have been plains for all that was visible of them. Out of the fog came the sounds of the hens and the sheep and the breathless gurgling of a little stream that hastened through the hoary grass.

The pony had not made a fresh hoof-print since the gipsy had slid from his back when the sun freed itself from the mantle of fog and showed a crimson disc beyond the mountains of Wales. The sky turned a pale blue like a tranquil lake and birds came from every tree and hedge to seek a grain of sustenance before the night.

But the night did not bring darkness. The full moon sailed out on the clear lake of the sky. Lord Ronald's shadow was black as a bat beside him. He bent his head to look, as though for the first time in his life he were conscious of it. The shadow turned away its head and the pony trembled in fear. An owl flew out of the hedge and began to strut up and down in front of him, dropping its wings and making low, tremulous sounds.

A thin hand touched his mane, then slid up over his cheek to his forelock. Fingers began delicately to draw out the burrs that clung there. As the burrs were dropped they did not fall straight to the ground but drifted, as though on a breeze, out of sight. Lord Ronald lowered his head and pressed it toward the fluttering hand. He gave a sharp whicker of delight.

Now he felt a bridle being put on him with a touch so caressing as to be almost unbearable. A bit was slipped into his mouth from which he sucked a new and dazzling power. He pawed the ground. He could scarcely wait for the thin legs to bestride him. He felt their taut pressure. He felt the familiar lift to the bridle and they were off !

The sheep ran to the farthest corner of the meadow, bundling themselves close together, baaing in consternation. This was not the pony they knew. This was a strange steed that flashed across the pasture scarcely seeming to touch it. As he flew he gave a neigh that echoed like a trumpet among the hills.

On the hills the russet bracken was crisp and the most delicate outlines shone in silver. On and on the humped hills unfolded themselves to the black mountains of Wales. The moon rose and sank. . . .

The Pony that would not be ridden

" That there pony's off his feed," observed the farm labourer next day.

" 'Twill do him no harm to fast a bit," answered Goslett but he went that afternoon to have a look at him.

Lord Ronald stood just where the gipsy had left him. It seemed that he had not moved from the spot where his small hooves were planted. He gave his usual look of beaming intelligence at the farmer. His nostrils were red as though he had been racing.

" 'Tis a pity you've such a bad nature," said Goslett, " for you're handsome, and no mistake."

He thought that the labourer must have pulled the burrs from his mane and groomed the mud away and he was surprised.

The next day the pony still refused to feed and stood in the selfsame spot. Goslett was glad that the gipsy was coming to-morrow to take him away.

But when to-morrow came and they went to the pasture he was not there. The fog was heavy and they plodded through it searching every corner, peering for breaks in the hedge. The sheep followed them in a body. There was a strange light in their yellow eyes, as though they knew something they wanted to tell.

THE NINTH LIFE

"HARRIET! Harriet! Harriet!" Her name
echoed through the pine woods. It echoed
across the water to the next island, was flung back
from its precipitous shore in a mournful echo. Still
she did not come.

The launch stood waiting at the wharf, laden with
the luggage attendant on the breaking up of the
holiday season. Summer was past, October almost
gone, wild geese were mirrored in the lake in their
flight southward. Now, for eight months, the Indians
and the wild deer would have the islands to themselves.

The Boyds were the last of the summer people to
go. They enjoyed the month of freedom at the end
of the season, when tourists were gone. They were
country people themselves, bred in the district. When
they were not living on their island they lived in a
small town at the foot of the lake, thirty miles away.
The year was marked for them by their migration to

the island in the middle of June and their return to winter habitation in October.

They were well-to-do. They owned their launch which now stood waiting at the wharf with the Indian, John Nanabush, at the wheel. He stood, dark and imperturbable, while Mrs. Boyd, her daughter and her cook raised their voices for Harriet. Mr. Boyd prowled about at the back of the cottage peering into the workshop, the ice-house, behind the wood-pile where freshly cut birch logs lay waiting for next year's fires. Now and again he gave a stentorian shout for Harriet.

They had delayed their departure for hours because of her. Now they must go without her. Mrs. Boyd came to the wide verandah where the canoe lay covered by canvas. She lifted the edge of the canvas and peered under it.

" Why, mother, what a place to look ! " said her husband. " The cat wouldn't be in there."

" I know," said Mrs. Boyd. " But I just feel so desperate ! "

" Well, we've got to go without her."

" And it's getting so cold ! "

On the wharf the girls wailed, " Oh, father, we can't leave Harriet on the island ! "

" Find her, Pat ! Find Harriet ! " said Mr. Boyd to the Irish terrier.

Pat leaped from the launch, where he was investigating the hamper of eatables, and raced up the rocky shore. In his own fashion he shouted for the cat. A chipmunk darted from the trunk of a jack pine, sped across a large flat rock, ran halfway up a flaming red maple and paused, upside down, to stare at the group on the wharf.

John Nanabush raised his soft, thick, Indian voice. "You folks go along home. I'll find Harriet. I'll keep her for you."

"That's a good idea," said Mr. Boyd.

"Harriet would never stay with John," said Mrs. Boyd. "She's devoted to us."

"Guess she'd rather stay with me than freeze," said the Indian.

"Will you promise to come back to the island to-morrow and search till you find her?"

"Oh, I'll find her," said Nanabush, in his comforting, sly voice. "We ought to be gettin' on now if you folks want to be home before dark."

"Pat! Pat! Oh, where is Pat gone?" cried the young girls.

Pat came bounding out of the woods, rushed at the launch, scrambled on board and sat there grinning.

"He's got some sense, anyhow," said the Indian.

"Sound the whistle, John," said Mrs. Boyd. "That might fetch her."

"What if she's dead!" cried the younger girl.

"You can't kill a cat," said Nanabush. He stretched out his dark hand and blew the whistle.

All eyes were turned to the woods.

The cook said, "I left a bowl of bread-and-milk for her by the back door."

"Come, mother," said Mr. Boyd, "it's no use. We can't wait any longer."

The launch looked like a toy boat as it moved among the islands. The reflection of the islands lay on the dark blue lake, more perfect than the reality. They were deserted.

It was only an hour later when Harriet came back. She was tired and hungry for she had been on a more strenuous hunt than usual. She had cut one of her feet and the hunt had been unsuccessful. She had curled up in the hollow of a tree and slept long, on the far side of the island. She had heard faint shouts for her but feline perversity had made her curl herself closer.

Now she circled the cottage, meowed outside the doors, leaped to the window-sills and peered into the rooms. There was a desolate air about it. She went to the wharf and saw that the launch was not there. The family would return in the launch.

She glided back to the cottage and found the bowl of bread-and-milk. She attacked it greedily but after a few mouthfuls her appetite left her. She began to wash her face, then to lick her coat to cleanliness and lustre. Her coat was a pleasing combination of tawny yellow and brown. She had a hard, shrewd face but there was affection in her.

The October sun sank in spectacular grandeur among the islands. There was no twilight. A blue, cold evening took swift possession. A few glittering stars were reflected in the lake. The air became bitterly cold and a white furry frost rimed the grass. Harriet crept into the canoe where Mrs. Boyd had lifted the canvas. There was a cushion in it. She curled herself up and slept.

At sunrise she leaped from the canoe and ran to the kitchen window. From its ledge she peered into the room. There was no fire. There was no cook. Harriet gave a faint meow of disappointment. She bent her acute sense of hearing to catch a sound of life in the cottage. All she heard was the whisper of little waves against the shore. Pointed leaves from the silver birches drifted in the golden air. It was very cold.

Harriet went to the bowl of bread-and-milk and began to eat it. She discovered that she was ravenous. But there was so much of it that she had to take breath before she could finish it. Even in her repletion she uttered a meow of longing. She was four years old and she had never been separated from the Boyds before. Her mother and her grandmother had belonged to the Boyds. She knew their movements and their life as she knew the pads of her own paw.

The bowl was emptied. As empty and hollow as the world in which she now found herself. Mechanically she began to wash her face, groom the fine hair behind her ears till it was erect as the pile of fine velvet. She stretched out her hind leg and swiftly licked the fur on the rim of her thigh. In this attitude it could be seen that she was with young. Her little teats showed rosy and fresh.

She heard a rustle in the fallen leaves and turned her green eyes defensively, fearfully, in that direction. A pair of porcupines stood staring at her, side by side, their quills upright, their yellow teeth showing in their trepidation. They had come to investigate the empty cottage.

Harriet gave a hissing scream at them, making her face as horrifying as she could. She stared, with her back to the kitchen door, screaming and making faces. The porcupines turned and ambled away, pushing into a dense growth of junipers.

An acorn clattered across the roof of the cottage and fell close to Harriet. She stood up, wondering what was coming next. The chipmunk that had watched the departure yesterday now looked over the eave at her. He knew she could not get at him where he was, but he longed to

retrieve his acorn. His neat striped head darted from side to side, his eyes questioned her. Her tail lashed its implacable answer. He put his little paw against the side of his face and settled down to watch her.

With a sudden leap she sprang toward the acorn, curved her paw about it, toyed with it. Beneath her fur her muscles flowed as she bent low over the acorn as though loving it, leaped back from it in disdain.

Paw to cheek, the chipmunk watched her.

Then, from all the empty world about her, her misery came to taunt her. She was alone, except for the helpless kittens that stirred inside her. She sank to her belly and gave a plaintive meow.

For a long while she lay with closed eyes. The chipmunk longed for his acorn. No other acorn could take its place. He kept elongating his neck to see into Harriet's face. She seemed oblivious of everything but he was not deceived. Still he could not resist. He darted down the wall of the cottage, made a dash for the acorn, snatched it.

He almost succeeded. But his nearness electrified her. In a flowing curve she sprang at him. He dropped the acorn and turned himself into wind and blew back against the wall of the cottage. From the eave he chattered at her. She stared out across the lake, ignoring him.

As the sun neared the tops of the pines she heard the delicate approach of a canoe. She ran to a point of rock and crouched there, among the junipers, watching.

It was John Nanabush come to look for her. The lake was very still and the reflection of canoe and Indian lay on the glassy water in silent companionship. He dipped and raised his paddle as though caressing the lake. He gave glittering diamonds to it from the tip of his paddle. He called, in his indifferent Indian voice : " Horriet ! Horriet ! You there ? "

She crouched, staring at him. She watched him with acute but contemptuous interest.

" Horriet ! Horriet ! " The canoe moved on out of sight behind a tumble of rocks but the Indian's voice still echoed dreamily.

She would not go with him ! She would not go. Surely there was a mistake ! If she ran very fast to the house she would find the family there. The cook would be there, frying fish for supper. Harriet ran in swift undulations up the rocky, shaggy steep to the cottage.

The chipmunk watched her approach from the eave, his little paws pressed together as though in prayer. But he reviled her shrilly.

She ran along the verandah and sprang to the sill of the kitchen window. Inside it was almost dark. There was no cook. The frying-pan hung against the wall. She heard the chipmunk scampering across the roof, in haste to get a good view of her. She sat down on the sill and opened her mouth but no sound came.

The chipmunk peered down at her, turning his striped head this way and that, quivering in his excitement. She lashed her tail but she would not look up at him. She began to lick her sore paw.

The red of the sky turned to a clear lemon colour. There was an exquisite stillness, as the trees awaited the first hard frost. An icy fear, a terrible loneliness descended on Harriet. She would not spend another night on the island.

As she ran to the water's edge she meowed without ceasing, as in protest against what she must do. A wedge-shaped flock of wild geese flew strong and sure against the yellow sky.

Before her the lake stretched dark blue, crisping in its coldness, lapping icily at her paws. She cried loudly in her protest as she walked into it. A few steps and she was out of her depth.

She had never swum before but she could do it. She moved her paws knowingly, treading the icy water in fear and hate. A loon skimming the lake was startled by her stark cat's head rising out of the water and swung away, uttering his loud, wild laugh.

The next island was half a mile away. The last sunlight was held in the topmost branches of its pines. It seemed almost unattainable to Harriet, swimming in bitter stubbornness toward it. Sometimes she felt that she was sinking. The chill all but reached her heart, still she struggled toward the blackness of the rocks.

At last the island loomed above her. She smelled the scents of the land. All her hate of the water and her longing for home tautened her muscles. She swam fiercely and, before she was quite exhausted, clambered up on the rocks.

Once there, she was done. She lay flattened, a bit of wet draggled fur. But her heaving sides and gasping mouth showed that life was in her. The wet hairs of her fur began to crisp whitely in the frost. Her tail began to look stiff and brittle. She felt the spirit going out of her and the bitter cold coming in. The red afterglow on the black horizon was fading. It would soon be dark.

Harriet had a curious feeling of life somewhere near. Not stirring, just sending its prickling essence in a thin current toward her. Her eyes flew open in horror of being attacked in her weak state. She looked straight into the eyes of a wild goose, spread on the rock near her.

One of his wings had been injured and he had been left behind by the flock, to die. He was large and strong but young. This had been his first flight southward. His injured wing lay spread on the rock like a fan. He rested his glossy head on it.

They stared at each other fascinated, while the current of his fear pricked her to life. She tightened the muscles of her belly and pressed her claws against the rock. Their eyes communed, each to each, like instruments in tune. She drew her chin against her frosty breast while her eyes became balls of fire, glaring into his.

He raised himself above his broken wing and reared his strong other wing, as though to fly. But she held him with her eyes. He opened his long beak

but the cry died in his throat. He got on to his webbed feet and stood with trailing wing, facing her. He moved a step nearer.

So, they stared and stared, till he wanted her to take him. He had no will but hers. Now her blood was moving quickly. She felt strong and fierce. His long neck, his big downy breast, were defenceless. She sprang, sunk her teeth in his neck, tore his breast with her hind claws, clung to him. His strong wing beat the air, even after he knew himself dying.

It was dark when she had finished her meal. She sat on the rock washing her face, attending to her sore paw. The air had grown even colder and snowflakes drifted on the darkness. The water in pools and shallows began to freeze. Harriet crept close to the body of the goose, snuggling warmly in its down. She pressed under its wing, which spread above her as though in protection.

She meowed plaintively as she prowled about the island next morning. The people who owned it had gone to their home, in a distant American city, many weeks ago. The windows of the cottage were boarded up. The flagstaff, where the big American flag had floated, was bare. Harriet prowled about the island, looking longingly at the mainland, filled with loathing of the icy water.

As she crept to its frozen rim she lifted her lip in loathing. A bit of down from the goose clung to her cheek. She crept on to the thin ice and, as it crackled beneath her, she meowed as in pain. At last, with a despairing lash of her tail, she went into

the lake and set her face toward the mainland. It was
three quarters of a mile away.

This ordeal was worse than last night's. The lake
was more cruelly cold. But it was smooth, stretched
like cold steel beneath the drifting snowflakes.
Harriet's four paws went up and down as though the
lake were a great barrier of ice she was mounting.
Her head looked small and sleek as a rat's. Her green
eyes were unwinking. Like a lodestone, the house
at the foot of the lake drew her. Her spirit drew
courage from the fire of its hearth.

A snake also was swimming to the mainland. Its
cold blood felt no chill. Its ebony head arched above
the steel of the lake. A delicate flourish on the steely
surface followed it. The two swimmers were acutely
conscious of each other but their cold eyes ignored.

Harriet scrambled on to the crackling ice at the
shore and lay prone. The life was all but gone from
her. She remembered neither food nor fire nor
shelter. The snake glided over the stones near her,
slippery and secure. She tried to rise but could
not.

The flurry of snow passed. A wind from the south-west made a scatteration among the clouds. They moved north and east, settling in grey and purple on the horizon. The sun shone out strongly, turning the October foliage to a blaze of scarlet and gold. The sunlight lay warm on Harriet's sagging sides.

She felt new life creeping into her. She raised her head and began to lick her sore paw. Then she ran her tongue in long eager strokes across her flanks. Her fur stood upright. Her flesh grew warm and supple.

She crept out on a rock, from whose crevices hardy ferns and huckleberry bushes grew. A few huckleberries glimmered frostily blue among the russet leaves. Harriet peered into the pool below the rock. She saw some small bass resting there in the watered sunshine.

She crouched, watching them intently. Her colours mingled with the frost-browned fern and bronzed leaves. She settled herself on her breast as though to rest, then her paw shot into the pool, her claws like fish-hooks drove into the bright scales. The bass lay on the rock, its golden eye staring up at her.

Now she felt refreshed and strong. She found the sandy track through the woods and trotted along it toward the foot of the lake. All day she pressed forward, meeting no one. She stopped only to catch a little mouse and eat it and rest after the meal.

At sundown a deer stepped out of a thicket and stood before her, his antlers arching like the branches

K

of a tree, his great eyes glowing. He looked at her then bent his antlers, listening. He raised a shapely hoof and stood poised. Harriet saw something shining among the leaves. There was a sharp noise. The shock of it lifted Harriet from her feet, made every hair of her tail vibrant.

The tall deer sank to his knees. He laid the side of his head on the ground and his great eyes were raised imploringly to the face of the hunter who came out of the wood. The hunter knelt by him as though in compassion. Then a stream of red gushed from the deer's throat. A dog came and sniffed his flank. Harriet peered down from a tree where she had hid. It was long before she dared go on.

She had gone only a short way when she saw a doe and a fawn, standing as though waiting. The doe lowered her head at Harriet but the fawn looked proudly aloof, holding its head, with the face innocent as a little child's, high on its strong neck. Harriet glided away, her paws brushing the snow from the dead leaves. She curled herself in a hollow in a tree and lay licking her sore paw. She thought of the dead deer's great body and the large pieces of flesh she had seen cut from it.

In the morning she was very hungry but there was nothing to eat. The sky was dark, the snow had turned to a rain that dripped from the trees and soaked her fur till it clung to her. But she ran steadily along the track, always drawn by the lodestone of the house at the foot of the lake. Passing toward it, she sometimes gave a meow as faint and thin as the fall of a pine needle. She ate a few blueberries from the dried bushes. She came to a space carpeted by glossy wintergreen leaves. She even ate some of the scarlet berries, eating them with distaste and curling lip but she was so hungry because of the kittens she carried. There seemed nothing living abroad except her.

The path crossed a swamp dense with a growth of cranberries. Beyond this she came to a settler's cottage, clean and neat, with poultry in a wire run. There was a hen turkey in the yard, followed by three daintily moving poults. A girl was milking a cow in an open shed. Harriet stood staring, lonely, hungry. She felt weighed down, almost too tired to go on.

A man came out of the house with a bucket. He saw her, and a piercing whistle brought two hounds. He picked up a stone and threw it. It struck her side.

Harriet turned into a fury, an elongated, arched, fiery-eyed, sneering fury. The hounds hesitated before her claws that reached for their eyes. She whirled and flew down the path. They came after her baying, sending up the volume of their voices in the rain. They urged each other on with loud cries. With her last strength she clambered into a tree and sat sneering down at them, her sides palpitating.

The hounds stood with their paws against the trunk of the tree, baying up at her. They changed places, as though that would help them. They flung themselves down panting beneath the tree, then

sprang up again, baying. But when the shrill whistle
sounded again they ran without hesitating back to
their master.

On and on Harriet limped over the rough track.
Sometimes she had a glimpse of the lake between
trees but she scarcely looked to right or left. The
homeward cord drew her ever more strongly. One
would scarcely have recognised the sleek pet in this
draggled tramp, this limping, heavy-eyed, slinking
cat.

She could see the twinkling lights of the town
across the bay when her pain came on. It was so
piercing, so sudden that she turned with a savage
cry, to face what seemed to be attacking her in the
rear. But then she knew that the pain was inside her.

She lay writhing on the ground and before long
gave birth to a kitten. She began to lick it, then
realised that it was dead. She ran on toward the
town as fast as she could.

She was still two miles from it when she had two
more kittens. She lay beside them for a while, feeling
weak and peaceful. Now the lights of the town
were out. Harriet picked up one of the kittens and
limped on. With it in her mouth she went along the
paved street. She gave a meow of delight as she
reached the back door of her own home.

She laid the kitten on the doorstep and herself
began limping back and forth, the length of the step,
rubbing her sides against the door. For the first time
since she had been left on the island she purred. The
purr bubbled in her throat, vibrating through her

nerves in an ecstasy of home-coming. She caressed the back door with every bit of her. She stood on her hind legs and caressed the door handle with a loving paw. Only the weak cry of her kitten made her desist.

She carried it to the tool-shed and laid it on the mat where the terrier slept in warm weather. She laid herself down beside it, trilling to it in love. It buried its sightless face against her lank belly. She lay flat on her side, weary to the bone.

But the shape of the kitten she had abandoned on the road now crept into her mind. It crept on silken paws with its tail pointed like a rat's and its eyelids glued together. Round and round it crept in its agony of abandonment, tearing her mind as its birth had torn her body. She flung herself on her other side, trying to forget it but she could not.

With a piteous meow of protest against the instinct that hounded her, she left the kitten's side and went out into the dawn. The rain had stopped and there was a sharp clear wind that drove the dead leaves scurrying across the frozen ruts.

The pain of her sore paw on the ice ruts was like fire but she hurried on, draggled, hard-faced, with the thought of the bereft kitten prodding her.

The dreadful road unrolled itself before her in an endless scroll of horrible hieroglyphics. She meowed in hate of it, at every yard. She covered it, mile after mile, till she reached the spot where she had littered. There, in the coarse wet grass, she found the kitten. She turned it over with her nose, sniffing it to see if

it were worth taking home. She decided that it
was.

Along and along the road she limped, the kitten
dangling from her unloving mouth, the dead leaves
whirling about her as though they would bury her,
the icy ruts biting her paw.

But the clouds had broken and the Indian-summer
sun was leaping out. As she hobbled into her own
yard her fur was warm and dry on her back. She
laid the kitten beside the other and gave herself up to
suckling them. And as they drew life from her, her
love went out to them. She made soft trilling noises
to them, threw her forelegs about them, lashed her
tail about them, binding them close. She licked their
fat bodies and their blunt heads till they shone.

Then suddenly a noise in the kitchen galvanised
her. She leaped up, scattering the sucklings from
her nipples. It was the rattle of a stove lid she
had heard. She ran up the steps and meowed at the
back door. It opened and the cook let out a scream
of joy.

" Harriet ! Harriet ! Harriet's here ! "

Pat ran to meet her, putting his paw on her back.
She arched herself at him, giving a three-cornered
smile. The cook ran to room after room, telling the
news. The Boyds came from room after room to
welcome Harriet, to marvel at her return.

" She must have come early last night," said the
cook, " for she's had kittens in the tool shed."

" Well, they'll have to be drowned," said Mr.
Boyd.

Harriet could not eat her bread and milk for purring. The purring sang in her throat, like a kettle. She left her saucer and went to Mr. Boyd and thrust her head into his hand.

"Just listen how she purrs!" said Mrs. Boyd. "I've always said she was an affectionate cat."

BOB

BOB was puzzled about a number of things but
the goings and comings of Bryanston puzzled
him most of all. One day Bryanston had gone to the
trouble of explaining to Bob that he had to leave him
so frequently because of business, very necessary business, and that he must be a good dog and not do things
to annoy the family, and that the time would soon
pass, and they would be together again.

Bob listened to all this without understanding a
word of it but he threw such a glow of understanding
into his golden eyes and the full dome of his cocker
spaniel's head looked so nobly receptive, that Bryanston
almost believed that he comprehended the lengthy
explanation. "You do understand, don't you, Bob?"
he asked.

What Bob understood was that the one he loved
was close beside him, making intimate pleasant-
sounding noises to him, laying a hand with cun-
ningly moving fingers on the sensitive back of his

neck. He pressed his shoulder against Bryanston's muscular leg, as a traveller might rest against a tree, and gazed upward into the shelter and strength of Bryanston's face.

Another thing that puzzled Bob was that no one in the house, excepting Bryanston, liked him. He liked everybody, though he loved only one. He even liked errand-boys, pedlars and tramps. He would meet them at the gate, welcome them with his feathered tail, sniff the various scents of them with the nostril of a connoisseur.

" What a fool he is ! " the family would say. " He is no earthly good ! "

The family consisted of Bryanston's father-in-law, his mother-in-law, his sister-in-law, his young brother-in-law, and his wife who was always ill. She would have liked Bob if she had seen more of him but she only heard of his misdemeanours ; how he had brought mud into the drawing-room on his big feet, how he had fleas and how he had dug a hole in the lawn to cool himself in.

One thing Bob was good for — in addition to being a fountain of pure affection — and that was shooting. Bryanston had never had a better gun dog. Their duck-shooting trips were a joy to them both. Each did his work so surely, so swiftly. The nights in a tent, on a bed of blankets laid over hemlock boughs when Bob lay with his head on Bryanston's thigh, were almost better than the days. Then Bob felt that they would never part again.

But how quickly the holiday came to an end !

How inevitably the life of partings and reunions began again ! Neighbours might have gauged the movements of the master by the behaviour of his dog. When Bryanston was away Bob spent his days on the lawn near the gate watching for the moment of return. When he saw Bryanston's stalwart figure, when he heard the heralding pipe of his whistle, Bob would sit for a moment motionless as though the joy were too much for him. Then Bryanston would call, " Aren't you coming to meet me ? " and Bob would run to him, crouching low in the humility of his love, uttering little yelps, as of pain.

From that moment they were only separated when Bryanston sat with his wife.

Early one spring new things happened to puzzle Bob. The house that had been so orderly, was being pulled to pieces. Strange men came, like big dogs, and began to tear the inside out of it.

Bob sat on the lawn and watched one piece of furniture after another being carried into a van. He wished Bryanston would come. He saw the canvas bag that held the blankets they took on their shooting-trips carried to the van and ran and sniffed it, barking loudly. He felt that somehow the barks might bring Bryanston. But no one paid any attention to him. He curled himself up on the lawn and laid the side of his head on his paws as though worn out by watching. He slept a little.

Suddenly, through the shuffling and tramping of the men, he heard the longed-for step. It moved deliberately toward him. Supple hands took hold of his ears. His being melted into delicious content. He snuffled Bryanston's hands and looked up into his master's face as though he would clamp him to himself for ever with that gaze.

After a while Bryanston brought a leather lead and snapped it on his collar. He looked up trustingly but he was puzzled. He was puzzled during the long walk. Bryanston walked quickly, never speaking to him. The sun was warm, the snow melting into rushing streams in the gutter.

They went into a strange house and Bob sat close to Bryanston's knee while the talk went on. The talk was about how you couldn't very well keep a spaniel in the city, especially when your wife's family didn't care about dogs and your wife was ill.

Then Bryanston went. He went so quickly that Bob could not get through the door after him. He sprang to the door and threw himself against it. The man of the house caught him by the collar and held him.

There was no hate or savagery in Bob. He did not try to bite the man. When he found himself held fast, when he found the door shut in his face, he stood still, trembling, and waited his chance to escape.

It did not come for two days.

He had refused food. He had sat quietly by the kennel where he was chained, waiting. At last they freed him.

He did not waste a moment. He trotted quickly in the direction of home but when he neared it he began to run wildly, his long ears flapping, his eyes strained.

The front gate was shut but he knew the loose board in the fence at the back and he passed through that. He trotted to the back door. It was shut. He ran to the front door. It was shut. He listened intently. The house was silent. He ran snuffling over every inch of the ground. There was no fresh scent of Bryanston.

He sat himself down in his accustomed place to watch the gate. A passing boy who knew him, called out :

" They're gone, Bob ! Don't you know that ? They're gone. You don't belong to them any more. You belong to the Grants. You go back to them, like a good dog."

Bob wagged his tail but he knew the boy was talking nonsense.

After a while he became troubled by the quietness of the house. He went into the street and began to seek the scent of Bryanston there. It tingled through his nerves like the warmth of the sun when he found it. He followed it, drinking it in with each breath, up one street, down another, till he reached the railway station.

The confusion, the clashing of trucks, the whistling of engines frightened him, but he thought he would find Bryanston there and he kept his dignity. He walked up and down the platform, up and down, threading his way among the confusion of boxes, bales and luggage but the scent was lost. He thought he had better go home.

He sat quietly on the lawn for a time ; then the

agony that was in him rose to his throat and he howled. He howled again and again in his mourning.

Toward evening Mr. Grant came and put a lead on him and took him back to his house. He was kind but Bob wanted Bryanston. He was very hungry and ate the supper that was set before him. He curled himself tightly in his kennel and felt the comfort of his long ears across his face.

The next day he went to his old home and from there to the railway station. He ran up and down the platform, snuffling eagerly. He tried to get on a train but was put off. Then he returned to the house and sat before the door, howling. The neighbours were disturbed. He made them miserable, sitting there in the snow and howling as though the end of the world had come. Once he sat through a blizzard, raising his desolate voice to the whirling snow, becoming as white as a snow dog. Boys made snowballs and threw them at him but after a look of reproach he returned again to his mourning.

Fortunately for him, this return of winter was brief. Soon it was really spring. Dandelions appeared like brass buttons on the green livery of the lawn. Newcomers moved into the house and Bob gave up hope of Bryanston's return there. He spent more time at the railway station. He knew exactly at what hours the trains left and he was almost always there to see them go. For some reason he gave no heed to the incoming trains. The men about the station liked him. They were proud to tell strangers of how faithful he was to Bryanston.

One day Bob knew he was late for the train. He ran along the road to the station, his long ears flapping, his short, feathered legs stretched in anxiety. Just as he ran on to the platform, he saw the train going out. Bryanston was standing on the steps of the last carriage. Bryanston was finishing a cigar and dropped the end to the ground.

Bob's astonishment was almost panic. For a moment he stood, as though turned to ebony. Then, with all the force that was in him, he strained to overtake the train.

Bryanston saw him coming. He had had to return to the town on business. The station-master had told him about Bob and he had hurried away, hoping the spaniel would not see him. He shrank from the pain of parting from him again, for Bob's sake. Now he saw Bob stretched to his farthest muscle — saw the wild flapping of his ears, the anguish of his starting eyes.

For a moment Bryanston closed his own eyes, hoping that when he opened them Bob would have given up the pursuit, be nothing but a small black image of a dog staring after the train.

But Bob had not given up hope when Bryanston looked again. He was straining harder than ever. Hope sprang in his heart like a tough-fibred weed that would not be uprooted.

Now he was hurling himself, with a strange rocking-horse motion ; he was staggering but he was not giving up. Before reason could stop him, Bryanston stepped inside the door of the carriage and jerked the

emergency cord that would halt the train. Then he took out his handkerchief and blew his nose. He stood with the handkerchief against his face, wondering what he would say to the conductor, as the train slowed down.

Bob could hardly drag himself to Bryanston. He felt himself picked up in the longed-for hands, laid against the familiar chest. He seemed to be all pounding heart, lolling tongue and glowing eyes.

" You can be fined for this ! " said the train officials.

" I know ! I know ! " said Bryanston. " But look at him ! Can you blame me ? "

All the way to the city Bob sat between Bryanston's legs, pressing close to him, feeling his nearness. Nothing else mattered. Nothing else mattered. . . .

Bryanston told the family about the reunion with Bob, with all the dramatic fire of which he was capable. His eyes shone as he told it ; but he felt uncomfortable at bringing the dog again to the house where he was not wanted. It was easy to see that they wanted Bob even less than before, though Bob wagged his tail whenever one of the family looked in his direction.

He found life very different here from what it had been in the house in the small town. Then there had been fields near by to run in. There had been country walks with Bryanston, walks to the lake and sticks hurled far out, to retrieve. In the background the shooting-trips, the free wild days and happy nights. Now Bryanston sat more and more with his wife when he was home. When he was away, Bob had nothing to do but sit on the front steps watching people go by. No one took him for walks. The weather was very hot. He was listless and he longed for a certain sort of grass. He could think of nothing but this particular grass.

He walked round and round the little garden, snuffing the plants, hoping to find what he wanted. He even went a long distance down the road, searching among the uncared-for growths of a vacant lot but he could not find it. He returned home and went in by the kitchen door. The maid offered him a chop bone but already she had given him too many bones. His appetite was gone but he was too polite to refuse. He took the bone and buried it deep in the geranium bed.

His paws and muzzle were earthy when he came into the house again. He wandered from room to room, searching for a cool spot. The door of the drawing-room stood open. It felt cooler in there. He sat down under one of the long lace window curtains, its creamy lace folds falling over his face so that he looked like a ridiculous canine bride.

It was the day of long lace curtains and formal best rooms.

For some reason Bob liked the feel of the lace over him. It felt cool and comforting. He sat still for a long while, enjoying it.

But again the urgent need for the particular grass troubled him. It came into his head that this stuff that hung over his face might do. He drew a bit of it into his mouth and began to chew. He chewed long and stubbornly, devouring as much of the curtain as he could.

For a time he sat hunched in an abyss of misery. Then he went into a corner and was sick on the carpet.

He had just lain down, feeling better, when the maid came in with her broom. " You brute ! " she exclaimed and hit him with the broomstick. He slunk swiftly out of the house.

Bryanston's brother-in-law was a nice fair curly headed young fellow. He hated to see the household upset by the presence of the spaniel. He made up his mind that he would get rid of him, swiftly and without fuss.

The next morning he whistled blithely to Bob as he lay on the porch. Bob looked at him, puzzled. It seemed too good to be true.

" I mean it ! " said the young man. " Come along, old fellow ! Good old Bob ! "

Bob leaped up and trotted at his heels. He had never been for a walk with this man before. He raised his head and waved his tail proudly. At the corner the young man stopped a street-car and they got on it together.

Bob sat at the young man's feet, gazing up trustfully into his face. The street-car joggled on and on. In the business part of the city, where the traffic was heavy in the narrow streets, the young man alighted and called to Bob. He walked quickly, with Bob close behind, up one crowded street, down another, through many side streets.

Then suddenly as they were about to cross a

street he darted ahead, reached the other side alone, stepped quickly on to a street-car and was gone.

Bob ran here and there among the legs of the passers-by, bewildered. He jostled against people, ran between a man's legs and almost overthrew him. He had never been in such a crowd before and it frightened him. He ran in a panic, forgetting to use the delicate sense that had been given him by nature, using only his troubled eyes.

At last he grew quieter. He put his nose to the ground. He found the scent he wanted, followed it across the street but there it disappeared. There was only blankness.

Up and down the street, dodging through the traffic, he searched. The policeman's eye was on him. A lost dog. A rough character tried to make up to him but Bob ran away. Now it was late afternoon.

Suddenly without warning a scent came on the air. Only the shadow of a scent, elusive, precious, promising. Bob stiffened. He stood stock still. His five senses were merged into one, like the five points of a star.

Now he did not hesitate ; he ran swiftly in the direction of home.

The family had just sat down to tea when Bob returned. He walked about the room waving his tail, lifting his lip in an apologetic smile. The young man came in for some chaffing.

When Bryanston arrived a few days later Bob met him joyfully at the door. But then, in a few minutes, came the news about the lace curtain.

Bryanston was shown it, tattered, disfigured. Bob had forgotten it in his joy and had run into the room with his master. Now he remembered and was swallowed up in shame. He abased himself at Bryanston's feet.

Bryanston later took him on his knees. He took one of Bob's silky ears in each of his hands. He kissed each ear in turn.

" This is the end, Bob," he said. " You've got to go."

Bob was not puzzled about this going as he had been about many things. He understood.

He sat beside Bryanston while the latter made ready a box with slats across the top and a layer of fresh straw on the bottom. He had had a good bath and been brushed till his coat shone. Bryanston wanted him to look his best when he arrived in the new home. Every time Bryanston's hand came near him, Bob touched it with his tongue.

When Bryanston lifted him into the box he sat still and resigned, looking at the dog biscuit and the big fresh bone lying in the corner. He trembled a little at the hammering of the slats. When they were in place Bryanston put his hand between them and laid it on the dome of Bob's head. Then Bob looked up at him from between the slats with his stricken soul in his eyes.

It was a long journey. All that afternoon and night, till noon of the next day, the train throbbed and beat along the hot rails. Bob did not touch the biscuit or the bone. He sniffed the air when the box was carried from the train to a waggon. There was a drive along a country road. He heard the bleating of sheep and the whicker of a colt.

" Isn't he a beauty ? " the new owner asked of his wife. Bob had finished a drink of cold water and stood looking up at them with a grave, searching look.

" Yes," she agreed, " but he has a sort of unfriendly look. I like to see a dog look friendly."

" Give him time," said her husband. " Mr. Bryanston thought the world of him and I dare say Bob misses him a bit. Bob's his name."

Bob knew this was his home. He investigated the garden. He lifted his head and faced the cool breeze that swept across the farm. At the edge of the lawn he found the sort of grass he liked. He took a blade of it delicately and walked on with it showing at the corner of his mouth.

On the farther side of the house he discovered a verandah and an old man sitting in a wheel-chair. This was the father of Bob's new owner. He had had a stroke years ago and his mind was dim. He was always happy and not aware that he was an unwanted burden in the house. When he saw Bob he laughed with pleasure.

" Hello ! " he said. " A dog, eh ? A gun dog ! A-shooting we shall go, eh ? I'm a devil of a shot ! Look here ! " He raised an imaginary gun to his shoulder and took aim.

" Bang ! A wild duck ! Over he went at the first shot ! Heels over head ! Retrieve him, boy — fetch him here ! "

Bob ran in the direction pointed to and searched in the long grass. He came back and looked up in the old man's face.

" Good dog ! Clever dog !" He took the imaginary duck from Bob's mouth. " What a dog ! Damn it, I'm glad you've come !" He stroked Bob's head with a shaking hand. He fished a toffee bull's-eye from his pocket and gave it to Bob. Bob ate it.

There was a benevolence about the old man, something pure and kind. Bob laid his chin on the woollen slipper that projected from the rug. He rolled his eyes toward the beaming old face.

" My goodness, what a dog ! Damn it, I'm glad you've come ! I was lonely, I can tell you ! "

Bob's tail beat the floor of the verandah.

CAT'S CRUISE

CAT was as black as a crow. This very blackness made her presence desired by sailors who were sure it brought them good luck. She was not pretty but she had charm which she had spent her life in exercising to get what she wanted. She was eight years old and she had woven into that eight years more travel and more adventure than most humans achieve in eighty. She had also brought forty-five kittens into the world.

She had been born on board a coaling-vessel, the *Sultara*, in the midst of a terrible storm when the crew thought that every moment would be their last. Her mother was ginger coloured; and she had, while the vessel floundered in distress, produced three ginger-coloured kittens besides this last one, black as the coal which formed the cargo. The stoker, looking gloomily at their squirming bodies, had growled :

" There'll be no need for us to drown *them*. The bloomin' sea'll do it ! "

He picked up the black midget and held it in his hand. He felt an instant's compassion for it. It had come out of darkness and was so soon to return ; yet there it lay, curved in his palm, bullet-headed, its intricate mechanism of tiny organs and delicate bones padded with good flesh, the flesh covered by thick silky fur, the whole animated by a spirit so vigorous that already ten little claws made themselves felt on his palm.

" If I could find a bottle the right size," he said, " I'd put you into it and chuck you into the sea. I'll bet you'd get to land ! "

But there was no need to try the experiment. Miraculously, it seemed, the storm began to abate. The waves subsided ; the vessel was got under control. One and all declared that they had been saved by the timely birth of the black kitten. It became the mascot, the idol of the ship.

They could not agree on a name for it. Some wanted a simple one, easy to say and descriptive of its colour, such as Smut, Darkie, Jet or Nigger. Others insisted on some name which would suggest the rescue of their lives by the kitten's timely birth. One offered Nick-o'-Time, with Nick for short. But they

could not agree. Then someone called her simply
" Cat," and the others, in spite of themselves, ac-
quiesced, as is often the case with names. From then
on she was proudly, affectionately, known as " Cat "
wherever she went.

She had a very round head, with small ears and
narrow, clear green eyes. She had exceptionally
long, glossy whiskers above a large mouth that
displayed needle-sharp teeth in a three-cornered smile
or a ferocious grin when her emotions were stirred.
Her tail was sleek and sinuous and almost never still.
Happy was the sailor round whose neck she wound it.
Her attentions were known to bring good luck.

As she grew up she reigned supreme on the vessel.
Nothing was too good for her. If what she wanted
was not given her at once, she climbed on to the
neck of the man who withheld it and put both arms
(you could not call them forelegs, because she used
them exactly like arms) round his neck and peered
into his eyes out of the narrow green slits of her own.
If he did not at once surrender, she pressed her stubby
nose on first one side of his face then on the other,
while with her claws she massaged the weather-beaten
back of his neck. If he were still obdurate, or perhaps
mischievous enough still to deny her, she reversed her
position and put her claws into his thigh. Gladly he
gave her then whatever she desired.

She had a loud vibrant purr and when she moved
gracefully along whatever deck she was favouring
with her presence, purring and swaying her long tail,
a feeling of reassurance and tranquillity came to all on

board. . . . It was a bitter thing to the crew of the coaling-vessel on which she had been born when, at the time of her first litter, she deserted them for a Norwegian schooner. The captain could scarcely persuade the crew to sail. The docks at Liverpool were combed for her without success. The voyage was one of rough weather and general dissatisfaction.

At that time the Norwegians had not heard of her. They had their own cat and did not want another. But she soon won them over and they had the most successful voyage they had ever known. When they next called at Liverpool the mate boasted of Cat in the hearing of one of the crew of the *Sultara*. He boasted of her intelligence, of her blackness, of the luck she brought.

On board the *Sultara* there was joy when they learned that she was safe, rage when they heard that she was living with the Norwegians. They visited the foreigners and saw for themselves the cat was " Cat." They found that she had a litter of ginger-coloured kittens. But the Norwegians would not give her up. They would give up one or all of her ginger-coloured litter but they would not give up " Katts."

The crew of the *Sultara* hung about the docks with scraps of kipper in their pockets, because Cat had a weakness for kippers ; but the Norwegians guarded Katt with terrible efficiency. When, however, she chose to go ashore, nothing could stop her. A morsel of kipper was proffered her at the right moment. She mounted the shoulder of the giver and was borne in triumph to her birthplace. She gave evidence of the greatest pleasure in her reunion with the crew who were ready to weep with joy at recovering her.

Cat remained with them for two voyages. Then again she disappeared, this time in favour of an oil-tanker bound for the East. . . . And so it went on, this life of change and adventure. She chose her ships. She remained on them till her love of variety prompted her to seek another lodging. But wherever she sailed she brought good luck and at regular intervals she returned to the *Sultara*. On all the Seven Seas she produced litters of ginger or grey kittens but never one of her own glittering black. She held herself unique. She was Cat.

Now, on a morning in late February, she glided down the gangway of the *Greyhound*, which had just limped into port after an Antarctic relief expedition. The voyage had lasted for six months and had been one of the mistakes of Cat's life, so far as her own pleasure was concerned.

The captain and crew of the *Greyhound* had been delighted when she sauntered aboard. The seal of success, they felt, had been set on the expedition. And they were right. The lost explorers had been discovered, living, though in desperate plight. Cat's reputation was still more enhanced.

But she herself was disgruntled through and through. She had never in all her years of travel experienced such a voyage. She felt disillusioned ; she felt ill. She felt like scratching the first hand that was stretched out to pat her.

"Hullo, Cat!" exclaimed a burly dock-hand. "So you're back from the Pole? And what captain are you going to sign up with next?" He bent to scratch her neck but she eluded him and glided off with waving tail.

"Cat don't look very bright," observed another dock-hand.

"She's fed up, I expect, with the length of the last voyage," said the first speaker, staring after her. "She don't generally go for such long ones. *And* the weather! *And* the grub! She could have done much better for herself and she knows it."

He turned to one of a crew which was about to sail for Norway.

"Hi, Bob! Here's Cat! Just back from the South Pole. P'raps you can make up to her."

Bob approached, grinning. He planted himself in Cat's way and held two thick tarry hands down to her.

"Puss, puss!" he wheedled. "Coom along wi' us. Tha can have whativer tha wants. Tha knaws me, Cat."

She knew Bob well and liked him. She suffered herself to be laid across his breast and she gave him a long look out of her narrow green eyes. He felt her ribs with his blunt fingers.

"She's naught but fur and bone," he declared.

"Her's been frettin' fer home," said the first.

"The sea is her home," said Bob. "But she's a dainty feeder. S'll I carry thee off, Cat?"

She began softly to purr. She relaxed in every

163

fibre. The tip of her tongue showed between her lips. She closed her eyes.

" She'll go with you," said the dock-hand and Bob began to pick his way among crates and bales, carrying Cat hopefully in his arms.

She heard the varied sounds of the docks, the shouts, the hoarse whistles of ships, the rattle of chains, smelled the familiar smells. It was music and sweetness to her after her long absence. She surrendered herself to the rhythmic movement of Bob's big chest.

In triumph he deposited her on his own deck. The rest of the crew stopped in their work for a moment to welcome her. The cook brought her a brace of sardines.

For politeness' sake she ate one but left the other on the deck. She arched herself against the legs of the first mate and gave her three-cornered smile. A ray of feeble sunlight struggled through the wintry fog and fell across her. She began to think she might sail with his crew.

" Keep an eye on her," said the mate to a cabin-boy. " Don't let her out of your sight till we're away."

All about was hurry and noise. Cat sat on the deck washing the oil of the sardine from her whiskers. The pale sunshine surrounded her but deep within her there was dissatisfaction growing. This was not what she wanted and soon it would be too late to return to the docks. She would be in for another long, cold voyage.

Her little round black head looked very innocent.

Her eyes were tight shut. Methodically she moved her curved paw over her face.

Someone called the boy and, forgetting the earlier order, he ran off. Cat was galvanised into life and movement. She flew along the deck. In another instant she would be on the docks. But Bob saw her and caught her in his huge hands. She liked him ; still she did not weaken. She thrust her claws into his hands and, with a yell of triumph and every hair erect, escaped.

It was some time before she regained her calm. She slunk among legs, among trucks, through scattered straw and trampled mud. The fog thickened again, settling clammily on her fur. It was bitterly cold. What she wanted was solitude. She was sick of the sight and sound of men and their doings.

She entered a warehouse and passed between tiers of wooden boxes and bales, stopping to sniff now and again when some smell attracted her. The cold in this building was very penetrating. Was she never to know warmth again ?

In a dim shed she found stalls, all empty except one in which a prize ram was awaiting shipment to America, where he was to be used for breeding. She clambered up the partition of the stall and perched there, gazing down at him. She did not remember having seen anything like him before. His yellow gaze was as inscrutable as hers.

With paws tucked under her breast she sat enjoying the sight of him. She stared at his massive woolly shoulders, his curly horns, his restless pawing hoofs.

He lowered his head and butted the manger in front of him with his hard skull. Cat felt that she could watch him for ever.

The gruff whistles of the ships shook the hoary air. The faint sunlight coming in at the cobwebbed window was shut off by a curtain of grey dusk. Cat and the ram were wrapped about by a strange intimacy. The chill increased. The docks became almost silent. The ram gave a bereft *baa* and sank to his knees.

Now he was only a pale mound in the dusk but Cat still stared at him. He was conscious of her too and, like some earth-bound spirit, he raised his yellow gaze to the glimmering stars of her eyes.

Toward midnight the cold became unbearable to her. On the Antarctic expedition she had slept in the bunk with a well-fleshed sailor. Now a thin rime was stiffening every hair of her coat. She rose stiffly and stretched. Her tail hung powerless. Some message, some understanding passed between her and the ram.

She leaped from the partition and landed between his shoulders. She sank into the deep oily warmth of his wool. He remained motionless, silent as the hill where he had pastured.

She stretched herself out on him with a purr of delight. She sought to feel his flesh with the fine points of her claws through the depth of his wool. A smell new to her rose from his body and the beginning of a *baa* stirred in his throat. Their two bodies united in the quiet breathing of sleep. Her sleep was light, of a pale luminous quality, always just on the edge of waking ; but his was dark and heavy, as though he were surrounded by shaggy furze and thick heather.

A dense fog rose from the sea at dawn and pressed thickly into the stall. With it crept a long grey cat with a white blaze on his face and his ears torn by fighting. He scrambled up the partition of the stall and peered down at the two below. He dropped to the manger and from there to the straw. He touched Cat tentatively.

She had been conscious of his approach. It had brought into her dreams a vague vision of a tawny striped cat she had met in Rio de Janeiro, where the relief ship had called. But the touch of the paw galvanised her. She gave a shriek and driving her hind claws into the ram's back, she reared herself and struck at the intruder's face as though she would put her mark on it for ever.

But he was not easily frightened off. He sprang to the ram's back also and through the fog Cat saw his white face grinning at her. He set his teeth in the back of her neck. They both shrieked.

The ram's deep, dark, warm slumber was shattered into fright. He bounded up with a clatter of hoofs, overthrowing the cats. His white eyelashes flickered. He glared in primeval rage and lowered his head to charge.

The cats scrambled agilely over the partition and dropped to the stone floor outside, their tails enormous. They sped in opposite directions into dim corners of the shed. The battering of the ram's head against the door of the stall echoed through the fog.

As Cat reached her corner a mouse flickered out of the gloom, squeaking in an agony of fear, and shot past her. With a graceful flourish of her limber body she turned completely round and captured the mouse with that one effective movement. She picked it up delicately in her teeth and crouched in the corner.

After a time the door opened and two men came in. They turned on a light and the interior of the shed was revealed in foggy pallor. The men entered the stall where the ram was. There came strange bumping sounds. The men cursed. Then they appeared leading the ram, roped by the horns. He was led out helpless, his little hoofs pattering on the stone floor. He uttered a plaintive, lamb-like *baa*. The men left the door open behind them.

Cat discovered the body of the mouse. It now meant nothing to her. She glided out on to the docks, wondering what ship she would sail in. She passed among them as they were dimly revealed, cargoes being loaded or unloaded, men working like ants. She felt a dim wonder at their activity, a faint disdain for their heaving bodies.

Toward noon, when a shabby blurred disc showed where the sun was, she came upon a passenger ship just departing on a West India cruise. She had never sailed on a passenger ship. They were an untrustworthy and strange world and she hated the sight of women.

As she stood pessimistically surveying it a kitchen worker tossed a slice of chicken-breast through a port-hole to her. She crouched on the pier devouring it while shivers of delight made her separate hairs quiver. She had not known that such food existed. After it was gone she sat beaming toward the porthole but nothing more was thrown out.

Luggage was being loaded on to the ship and a throng of people, of a sort she had never before seen, hastened up the gangway. One of them, a man, bent and gently massaged the muscles in the back of her neck, before he passed on. She beamed after him. She had not known such hands existed, so smooth, so tender. They were like the breast of chicken she had just devoured.

She rose, chilled by the clammy cold, and glided up the gangway on to the ship.

She knew that she was a stranger here and some instinct told her that quite possibly she might not be welcome. She slunk along the innumerable white passages, making herself as nearly invisible as possible. She glanced in at the doors of staterooms as she passed. Generally there were women inside and sometimes the rather disgusting smell of flowers was on the air.

Cat heard the thunder of the whistle. She felt a quiver go through the ship. She had a mind to get off it while there was yet time but she felt powerless to turn herself away from the delicious warmth that was radiated from every corner of the liner. It made her feel yielding, soft. She wanted something cosy to lie down on.

She paused at the door of a cabin that was empty except for the promise of a man's coat and hat thrown on the berth. She went in and walked round it, purring. She held her tail stiffly erect, all but the tip which moved constantly as though it were, in some subtle way, gauging the spiritual atmosphere of the cabin.

Gregg, the swimming-instructor, found her there curled up on his coat. They had left the docks so she could not be put ashore. He recognised her as the cat he had caressed and supposed that she belonged on the liner. He tucked her under his arm and carried her to the kitchen quarters. The boy who had thrown her the morsel of chicken recognised her. He had once been galley-boy on an oil-tanker she had favoured with her presence.

"It's Cat," he explained. "'Aven't yer never 'eard tell of Cat? W'y, we're in luck, mister! And yer ought to be proud to share your berth wiv 'er!"

But Gregg did not want to share his berth with Cat, even after he had heard her history and virtues. He dumped her down and rather glumly retraced his steps. He felt a shrinking from the long cruise that stretched ahead of him. To be sociable was a part of his job and he hated the thought of sociability.

He had, in fact, seen too much of people. He had had more experience of society than was good for him. He was not yet thirty but he had lost a fair-sized fortune, the woman he loved and, worst of all, his hope and fortitude. He had been at his wits' end to find a job when a friend had got him this post as swimming-instructor. He was in a state bordering on despair but, here he was, bound to seem cheerful and gay, to take a passionate interest in the flounderings of fat passengers in the pool.

No one on board was so out of sympathy with the cruise as was he. Indeed, everyone on board was in sympathy with the cruise but Gregg and Cat, who did not at all understand cruising for pleasure.

She was there in his berth waiting for him when he returned to his cabin that night, having found her way through all the intricacy of glittering passages. He was a little drunk, for he was very attractive and people insisted on treating him. The sight of Cat lying there on his bed angered him. He was about to put her out roughly when she rolled over on her back, turned up her black velvet belly and round little face with the glittering eyes narrowed and the three-cornered smile showing her pink tongue. He bent over her, pleased in spite of himself.

" You're a rogue," he said. " But you can't get around me like that."

For answer she clasped her forepaws round his neck and with her hind paws clawed gently on his shirt front. She pressed her face to his and purred loudly in his ear.

" Cheek to cheek, eh ? " said Gregg, and gave himself up to her hypnotic overtures.

Morning found them snuggled close together. He sent the steward for a dish of milk for her. He appeared at the swimming-pool with her on his shoulder. She basked in the heavenly warmth of the place.

From that time she spent her days by the pool. Tolerantly, almost benignly, she watched the skill or awkwardness of the swimmers. When the pool was deserted she crouched by its brink gazing at her reflection, dreaming of lovely fish that might have graced it. At night she slept with Gregg. She thrived immensely.

When they were in sparkling southern waters, Cat disappeared early one evening. She met Gregg at the door of his cabin with a tremulously excited air. She advanced towards him, purring, then turned her back and flaunted her sinuous black tail. She looked back at him over her shoulder. Her head and tail met. She caught the tip of it in her mouth and lay down on her back, rolling coyly from side to side. She looked strangely slender.

"So you've been and gone and done it," said Gregg. "Not on the bed, I hope!"

No, not on the bed. In the wardrobe, where Gregg's soft dressing-gown had somehow fallen from its peg. There were three of them, all plump, all tawny, like the gentleman in Rio de Janeiro.

Next day Gregg got a nice box with a cushion and put the kittens in it. He carried them to the balmy warmth of the air that surrounded the swimming-pool, and all the bathers gathered to admire and stroke them. They were the pets of the ship. But Cat cared only for Gregg. She fussed over him far more than she did over her kittens. She refused to stay with them by the pool at night, so the box had to be carried to his cabin. There she would sit waiting

for him, her glowing eyes fixed on the door, every nerve tuned for his coming.

But on one night he did not come. She waited and waited but he did not come. At last she sprang up from suckling her kittens, and they fell back like three tawny balls. The door was fixed ajar. She glided through the opening and began her search for him.

The smoke-room was closed; the lounge was empty, the decks deserted except for a pacing figure in uniform. At last Cat saw Gregg standing, still as a statue, in a secluded corner where a lifeboat hung. Silent as the shadows cast by moonlight, she drew near to him. But she did not rub herself against his leg as usual. She climbed into the lifeboat and over its edge peered down into his face.

That night Gregg felt alone — lost. In spite of the moonlight, the myriad glittering waves, the world was black to him. The life on this luxurious liner, among these spoiled shallow people, was suffocating him; he could not breathe. He looked back on his own life as a waste, on his future with despair. He had made up his mind to end it all.

Cat watched him intently as he leaned against the rail. If he had been her prey she could not have observed him with more meticulous concentration as he mounted it. Just before he would have leaped over the side she sprang on to his shoulders with a shriek that curdled the blood of those whose staterooms gave on that deck. She not only shrieked but she drove every claw into Gregg. She turned herself into a black fury whose every hair stood on end, whose eyes glared with hate and fear at that gulf below. . . .

" I don't know what the devil is the matter with her," Gregg said to the officer who hastened up. " She's as temperamental as a prima donna." His hand shook as he stroked her.

But she had saved him from his black mood, saved him from his despairing self. When he was undressed, he looked in wonder at the little bloody spots on his shoulders. . . . Cat slept on his chest.

He made up his mind that he would never part with her. He owed her a debt which could only be repaid by the certainty of affection and gentle living for the rest of her days. He would find lodgings where she would be welcome.

But Gregg reckoned without Cat. By the time they reached port she was sick to death of the luxury liner. There was not a smell on board that pleased her. She liked Gregg but she could do without him. She liked her three plump kittens, but the quality of real mother love did not exist in her. She loved the sea and the men who spent their days in strenuous work on the sea. She disliked women and scent and all daintiness. She was Cat ; she could not change herself.

In the confusion of landing no one saw her slip ashore. She vanished like a puff of black smoke. It was as lovely a morning as any they had seen on the cruise. The air was balmy, the sky above the dock blue as a periwinkle. When Cat reached the places she was accustomed to she purred loudly and rubbed herself against tarry trouser-legs, arched her neck to horny hands. But she was coy. She would not commit herself. For a fortnight she lived on the dock, absorbing the satisfying smells of fresh timber, straw, tar, salt fish, hemp, beer, oil and sweat. She even renewed acquaintance, this time more amiably though with loud screams, with the grey-furred gentleman who had called on her in the ram's stall.

At last she sailed on a cattle ship, and all her past was as nothing to her !

PETER — A ROCK

YOUNG Ffolkes did not want to call the puppy Peter. He would have liked something quite unusual and distinctive or absolutely common-place, such as Jack. He thought it rather hard that he was not allowed to name his own puppy. On the other hand he was so grateful to the seventeen ladies who lived at Mrs. Dowling's for tolerating the dog in their midst that he would have consented to name him Cyril or even Claud.

Mrs. Dowling herself, handsome and accustomed to having her own way, said that Peter was a good name and just suited him. He was in truth rather a Peterish sort of puppy, playful, appealing, whimsical. He had just reached the long-legged stage and his tail was turning into a silky, wavy plume. There was a shallow sparkle in his hazel eyes. He had been sired by the champion Scotch collie, Glen Robert.

Young Ffolkes often wondered why he lived at Mrs. Dowling's. It was certainly an odd environment for a lively chap of twenty-seven. It had begun by his going there with his mother for a year, after she had given up housekeeping. And later, when she had died, it had seemed the natural thing for him to return to the midst of these middle-aged and elderly ladies who had known her — a few of whom had been old friends and were full of sympathy for him.

Now he had lived there for five years. Some of his young lady friends began to wonder if he were not altogether too comfortable at Mrs. Dowling's and might not spend the rest of his days there.

He was indeed very comfortable. He had a big sunny room on the top floor at the front, with a coal grate, two wicker armchairs and three stuffed ones, also an enormous shabby couch which even the attentions of a half-grown puppy could not disorganise. The two rooms underneath were occupied by Miss Green who was just hard enough of hearing not to be troubled by noises overhead.

Young Ffolkes had seen changes at Mrs. Dowling's. He had seen Miss Green's head turn from iron-grey to snow-white. He had seen Miss Hubbard change from a plump woman into a very fat woman. He had watched old Mrs. Slee grow prettier and prettier and old Mrs. Kane grow uglier and uglier.

All the ladies were interesting to young Ffolkes. As he read his morning paper he would pause in his perusal of sports news or political probings to hear what Mrs. Forrester was saying to Miss Hubbard about Miss Kenny who was in hospital after an operation for gallstones. Or perhaps what Miss Green was saying to Mrs. Slee about the quarrel between the Low Church rector and the High Church organist. Almost all the scraps of conversation over-heard from the eight small tables at Mrs. Dowling's were concerned with either church or hospital.

Young Ffolkes found their interest in his own affairs almost overpowering at times. If he were late to breakfast on a week-day morning there was a distinct feeling of apprehension in the room and a flutter of relief stirred their open newspapers when he entered and took his seat at his own small table behind the door. There was no knowing what a young man of his spirit might not get led into in a large city.

The front door was locked early at Mrs. Dowling's and it was a rule of the house that any of the guests who stayed out late should lay a slip of paper on the table in the hall informing the parlourmaid of the fact so that she might stay up to let them in. Young Ffolkes had often a sneaking sort of feeling when, night after night, he laid his slip of paper bearing the words — " Mr. Ffolkes will be out late " — on the hall table. Each one of the ladies read this slip, not with disapproval, as he imagined, but with a certain exhilaration. It was almost as though she were out with him herself.

On the occasional nights when he had a little poker party in his own room and his friends gave vent to loud masculine guffaws he felt distinctly anxious for fear the ladies should be disturbed in their sleep. But, if they were, it was only to smile indulgently and think — " What a good time young Ffolkes is having to-night ! "

They were the kindest lot of women imaginable. In all the five years he had lived among them he had never heard a mean or sneering remark, though occasionally their patience was almost exhausted by Miss Hubbard's excessive use of the telephone.

Everyone was, in short, extremely comfortable at Mrs. Dowling's. The seventeen female guests were no longer hampered by husbands or other male hangers-on who might have interfered with them, and the only man among them was their darling.

But, from the time Peter arrived on the scene, he had his share of their devotion. His vitality and his ceaseless expression of it were a wonder and delight. At first young Ffolkes arranged that Peter should spend his days in a kennel with a small wire enclosure about it and his nights in a dog-basket at the foot of Ffolke's bed, but it was impossible to carry out that arrangement for any length of time.

It was lovely autumn weather. A group of the ladies stood about the kennel gazing down at Peter who, on hind legs, pawed the barrier between him and them and threw all his puppy soul into his cajoling eyes.

" Poor little fellow ! " said Mrs. Forrester. " It does seem hard to be shut in there."

" How he wriggles ! " said Miss Green.

" Peter, Peter, nice little Peter ! " exclaimed Mrs. Kane who had been the first to suggest his name. She put her hand on his head and in an instant he had given it a playful gnaw, then kissed it and covered it with slobber. But she did not mind. There was something in the feel of that agile wet tongue !

" Poor little soul ! " she said, wiping her hand on her handkerchief. " He is so terribly lonely ! "

Bereft of her hand Peter began to bite the wire-netting, his teeth of a marvellous whiteness and his gums of a marvellous firm pinkness. He made sounds that were half whine, half panting and wholly imploring.

" I'm going to have him out of there for a bit," said Miss Hubbard, dictatorially.

She bent over, took him under the armpits and lifted him out.

Scarcely had his feet touched the close-mown lawn when he set off in a mad circling of joy. Round and round and in and out among the ladies he whirled, uttering glad yelps. He leaped upon Miss Hubbard and left paw-marks all down her front. He caught Mrs. Forrester by the ankle and made a ladder in her new silk stockings. He gave such a tug at Mrs. Kane's skirt from behind that she all but sat down on him. Then he took a flying leap over the geranium bed.

"Peter! Peter!" screamed the ladies in unison and they ran after him as they had not run in twenty years.

With a wave of his tail he fled before them. He sped along the concrete walk that led to the street where tram cars, motors, and lorries thundered past. He headed for certain destruction and might have suffered it had not Mrs. Slee, going out to make a call, seen him and heard the cries.

Light as a girl she ran after him and caught him by his plumy tail just as he reached the kerb and a truck-driver stuck his head out of his window, shouting, "Here, you, look after yer dawg!"

Mrs. Slee returned triumphant, with Peter's back against her chest, and faced Peter's baffled liberators.

"I saved his life!" she said firmly. "He would have been utterly smashed if it had not been for me!"

"He would," they all agreed but Miss Hubbard and she hung her head.

"He was so pathetic," she said, "and he is such a puppy!"

"Well," repeated Mrs. Slee, "I saved his life, but I shall not say anything about it to Mr. Ffolkes."

Peter, with a swift undulation of his body, turned his face toward hers and licked it gratefully. His tail beat against her thighs.

After that the ladies satisfied themselves by presenting Peter with rubber bones, rubber balls and arrowroot biscuits in his enclosure but every evening young Ffolkes took him by the scruff and lifted him on to the lawn when at least half a dozen of the seventeen ladies were always there to watch and encourage his mad gambollings. Sometimes Henry the cook gave him a bit of freedom and many a surreptitious meal from the kitchen in spite of Ffolkes's orders to the contrary. Peter was consistently overfed and fed the wrong thing but his activities were such and his mad spirits were such that his gastric juices flowed like the wind.

As the winter came on Peter spent less and less time in his run. Henry often took him into the kitchen for warmth and from there he found his way into the hall. The ladies with one accord agreed that the dining-room was no place for him. When he showed his nose there, there was a chorus of, " Out, Peter ! Out, naughty dog ! " in tones varying from Mrs. Slee's high refined voice to Miss Hubbard's deep rough one. He would grin sheepishly at them, wave his tail and back away. Finally he took to lying on the large sofa in the hall, opposite the door of the dining-room, through which he surveyed them with the lofty air of a Sultan appraising his harem.

Occasionally, very occasionally, only when the door at the end of the passage was shut and he could not find his way out in time, he went into the drawing-room and made a puddle in the dark corner behind the piano.

Mrs. Forrester who always played a little on the piano directly after lunch — Mendelssohn's Consolation if the lunch were not so good as usual ; a Strauss waltz if it were better than — invariably discovered the mishap.

She would throw up her hands and exclaim :

" Peter has made a puddle ! "

" How many times is this ? "

" It is the third time."

" No — there was that other time — right in the middle of the room — this is the fourth."

" Nonsense ! I counted that. This is the third."

Then another voice, " I have kept count absolutely. This is only the third ! "

" But you all keep forgetting the time in the very middle of the room."

" I *think* I am able to count up to *three*."

" Oh, well, if you're going to be annoyed——"

" I'm not annoyed."

" Of course, none of us are annoyed——"

" But I don't like to see the poor little fellow blamed for what he hasn't done."

" The point is that he ought to be whipped."

" Shall we tell Mr. Ffolkes ? "

" Heavens, no ! "

They were all agreed on that point.

The object of the discussion lay flat on his back looking wistfully up into the faces above him, his paws drooping above his upturned snow-white belly, his plumed tail waiting to be released into activity. He could gauge to a nicety the moment when it was proper for him to roll over on to his feet and act as though nothing had happened while Alice, the parlourmaid, mopped up the puddle.

Peter — A Rock

In the spring Peter was a year old and had developed a new dignity and repose. He no longer chewed up cushions or carried his master's slippers downstairs or dragged intimate garments belonging to the ladies on to the landing. He became fastidious in his habits and in his person, showing distinct pride when his master had given him a bath and an extra good grooming. He would sit for hours on the porch watching the passing traffic or escorting each of his seventeen ladies to the corner, when they walked out, and meeting them on their return. But he reserved a special welcome for young Ffolkes, rushing at him with joyous barks when his slight figure separated itself from a group alighting from a tram. He went into the house and upstairs with him to their room. He displayed the room to him with confidential glances, as though saying, " I have guarded this for you all day. Now it is yours and mine to enjoy."

But, though Peter was on confidential terms with his master, he felt no great love for him. Ffolkes to him was just a different sort of lady guest, stronger, more intimate and rather more precious because he was away so much. Even when they went on their evening walks together or on Sunday tramps outside the city, he escorted young Ffolkes very much as he escorted the other guests.

Ffolkes felt this lack in their comradeship and it troubled him because, when he had acquired Peter, he had been confident of a special great love between them.

He would take Peter's long fine head between his

hands and gaze into his shallow dancing eyes and say, almost reproachfully, " There are just two of us, old man, just the two of us. . . ." But Peter would look back at him with a jocular air, fetch his ball and encourage young Ffolkes to romp.

It was not till the summer holidays that the great love came. One by one the ladies drifted away to the pleasant places where they spent the hot weather. Of the seventeen only three were left and they the least interesting to Peter. The house was quiet, the weather hot. He had never had so little appetite. He even discovered that he had got fleas and fussed over them night and day.

Then August came and young Ffolkes's holidays. He had a whole month this year because he had taken on a good deal of responsibility in the past months and badly needed the rest.

He spent the first day in shopping for a trip to the North. He had hired a tent and a canoe and he bought a second-hand car. He was so excited when he came home that night that he snatched up Peter in his arms and hugged him till it hurt. Peter gave a hilarious bark and, when he was put down, shook his cushion as he had not shaken it for months.

The next day he could scarcely believe his eyes, or his ears, or any of his five exquisitely acute senses.

In the first place young Ffolkes did not go away after breakfast as usual. Yet it was not his Sunday way of staying at home. He behaved quite differently. Right after breakfast he began stowing things in boxes while Peter looked on grinning and once, just to be in the game, dragged one of the garments out again. He got a playful cuff for this. Then, when all was packed and carried down the two flights of stairs to the hall, Ffolkes disappeared for a space. But Peter knew he was coming back and sat guarding the luggage with a grand possessive air.

When young Ffolkes reappeared it was at the wheel of his own new car. He was bareheaded and all his wiry mouse-coloured hair stood on end. There was colour in his usually pale cheeks. He jumped out and began piling in his belongings. Peter never left his side.

" Now," exclaimed Ffolkes, " in you get, old man ! Our own car ! Yours and mine ! And mind you don't fall out."

Peter braced himself on the seat. He took his place with assurance. Whatever he was in for, he was in for it with a whole heart. Mrs. Dowling, the three remaining guests and Alice, the parlourmaid, waved good-bye from the steps. Peter raised his voice and barked.

" Isn't he the proud one ? " cried Alice.

The dry hot air of the city was left behind and they were gliding along the country road where they had often walked on a Sunday. Peter's eyes roved over the fields, his nostrils quiveringly drew in the exciting scents. He pressed his nails into the seat of the car, making sure of his hold. Now and again Ffolkes's hand stole from the wheel and buried itself in the depths of Peter's snow-white ruff.

But after a while there was nothing familiar to be

seen. They passed through villages where dogs ran out and barked at them and were ignored by Peter. They went up hill and down hill and at last, at the edge of a little wood where a spring glimmered, the car was drawn up and they got out for lunch.

Never before had they had their meal on the ground together. At first, because the food was laid on the grass, Peter thought everything was for him and circled excitedly about trying to decide what he should attack first. But he soon discovered that the meal was to be shared and settled down to devour the enormous mixed collation donated by Henry. But before he could eat he must drink. He had never been more thirsty. He thrust his muzzle into the cold spring and drank till he could drink no more. Young Ffolkes had scarcely begun when Peter was gnawing the marrow from his bone.

They went on and on. In late afternoon the country became wilder, the farms more scattered. There were great dark woods and now and again a rabbit scurried across the road. Peter trembled with excitement. He could not settle down to rest though his legs ached from his strained position. The air had become cool, with strange enticing scents in it.

They stopped and had tea, then went on. " We must get there before nightfall," said Ffolkes.

They did. In a wildly beautiful spot beside a darkly shining lake he turned the car from what had become no more than a rough track, on to the crunching white gravel of a beach. There, a white pyramid in the dusk, rose their tent. On the fine sand, on the water's edge, lay their canoe. A man came out of the tent.

"I've got everything ready for you, sir. I began to think you'd lost your way."

"Thank goodness, I didn't do that! I made pretty good time considering it's my first long drive. But I should never have found this place after dark." He looked about him, exhausted but happy.

While Ffolkes carried the things into the tent the man lighted the fire he had laid on the beach. Quiet little flames crept in and about the dry twigs and driftwood, then leapt up quick and alive and crackled and blazed in the dusk.

Peter moved warily about, investigating all. He had been transported into a life so new, so strange, he could not comprehend it. Yet through all his sensitive being there was a wild response to this strangeness. It was as though he had come home, to a home that was not known to him, yet was of his essence.

The man, having done all that was needed, stepped into a canoe and with a few practised strokes slid swiftly from the beach. Peter stood at the water's edge watching him go.

"That's a fine collie you've got," called the man. "He'll have a good time here."

"Yes," answered Ffolkes. "He's a good dog." He came to the water's edge and squatted beside Peter.

"Are you a good dog, Pete?" he murmured. "Are we going to have a good time? Lord, I'm tired, and so happy I don't know what to do!"

The first thing he did was to have a swim. Peter had seen him in the bath before but never such a bath as this ! Ffolkes stood straight and white in the firelight for a moment, then ran swiftly out into the water and plunged.

Peter stood bewildered, half frightened. He uttered little reproachful whines. Then, when he saw his master's arms breasting the deep darkness farther and farther from shore, he gave a succession of agonised barks that ended in a howl.

"Come on, come on, Peter, you dud ! " cried Ffolkes.

Peter ran into the water a little way, then back to the shore, barking more wildly than ever.

"Come along, Peter, you mug ! " cried Ffolkes.

Before he realised it or quite knew what he was doing, Peter found himself in that deep, cool wetness, paw over paw, muzzle held up, straining toward the white, loved form. For in that moment he discovered he loved young Ffolkes and did not want him out of his sight.

Now a new life began for the two. They were alone together, isolated as though the only people on earth, except for the man who reappeared twice each week bringing bread and meat and fruit. Sometimes they heard a distant shout or the throb of a motor launch, but these sounds meant no more to Peter than the cry of the loon or a far-off roll of thunder.

They woke early in the chill pine-scented stillness of their tent, stretched, yawned, romped for a bit before they rose and went out into the sun. Then

came the race to the lake, the joyous plunge and the swimming side by side. While Ffolkes fried the bacon over the fire on the beach, Peter ran like a young wolf through the woods, chasing wild things, intoxicated by this sudden spacious freedom.

He learned to sit motionless as a statue in the stern of the canoe. They explored the shores of the lake and made expeditions up winding little rivers half hidden in the forest. He learned to go about his own business while Ffolkes stood on a jutting rock fishing for bass. Once he surprised a deer and her fawn and chased them for miles, not returning till evening, tired out and smelling of bracken.

" Don't do that again, Pete," begged Ffolkes. " You gave me a terrible fright."

All his former life faded from Peter's mind. The seventeen ladies at Mrs. Dowling's were as though they had never been. He and young Ffolkes were gods who would continue in this noble round for ever.

But August drew to an end. The sunlight took on a yellowish tone, the bracken dried and there came the smell of distant forest fires. Young Ffolkes packed his boxes and stowed them in the back of the car.

They stayed up late that night, sitting close together before the fire that turned the branches of the towering pines to burnished metal and showed young Ffolkes's face and arms of a rich bronze. He held Peter close to him.

" It's been a great time, old man," he said, " and we'll do it every year — you and I — as long as we live." Under his hand he felt Peter's heart beating, ardent and strong.

A number of the ladies had returned from their holiday when dog and master walked into Mrs. Dowlings's. There were exclamations of astonishment at the young man's coat of tan and delight at Peter's size and beauty.

He had indeed developed into a noble-looking dog. The shallow sparkle had left his eyes and in its place there was a steady glow of pride and race. When he raised them to young Ffolkes's face they were filled with an abiding love and confidence.

Now he remembered the routine of the day at Mrs. Dowling's. He accepted the return to it without dismay. He knew that the time would come when he and the one person who was now necessary to him would again find the forest and the lake.

He stalked about the garden investigating each remembered corner. Without effort he leaped over the wire fence of his run and put his long nose disdainfully into his kennel and leaped out again. When Henry brought him a large juicy bone between meals, he waved his tail in thanks, guarded it for a decent space, then buried it among the shrubs. When the ladies offered him sweets and bits of cake, he ate them good-humouredly but without enthusiasm. All his senses were concentrated on the return of Ffolkes from the bank.

They had been back only three days when the news of Ffolkes's promotion came. When he entered the dining-room that night several of the ladies noticed his unusual aspect. If a man can, at the same moment, look both elated and depressed, Ffolkes did. In the drawing-room after dinner he told them he had been transferred to an excellent position in the London branch of his bank. What almost spoiled his pleasure was that he would not be able to take Peter. No dog might enter England without enduring a quarantine of six months. Ffolkes could not think of that for Peter. It would break his spirit. Besides, what should he do with him in London ? Young Ffolkes's bronzed forehead was creased with anxiety.

Mrs. Dowling offered to keep Peter. All the ladies would be so kind to him. But Ffolkes could not contemplate such a life for him now. Peter was grown up. He was a man's dog.

Then Pryce came forward. He was the manager of the bank where Ffolkes was employed. Ffolkes had been to his house several times, had admired Pryce's pretty wife and two attractive children. The children would love to have a dog. Every summer they went to the country and that would be good for Peter.

So one evening young Ffolkes drove his car to the Pryces' house, with Peter sitting very upright beside him. Ffolkes's heart was as heavy as lead.

" Gosh," he thought, as he turned into the drive, " if I had known it would be like this I don't believe I should have taken the job ! "

The children, Joan and Kenneth, made a great deal of Peter. Pretty Mrs. Pryce exclaimed at his beauty and Pryce told young Ffolkes not to worry, that they would give Peter the very best care possible.

And so they did, according to their understanding, after the first days when he would have nothing done for him but sat, still as though carved, watching the door, waiting for young Ffolkes's return ; rejecting all food ; refusing, with threatening lip, to be touched ; refusing to take exercise. He was a symbol of calm patience, trusting the awaited footstep, waiting to leap into joyful activity.

A leather armchair that Ffolkes had sat in on the night he had brought Peter to the Pryces', Peter now appropriated. He sat in front of it all day long, sometimes resting his long head on the seat. He curled up in at night. When the children teasingly touched the chair he gave a low growl that made Mrs. Pryce exclaim to her husband :

" I wish you had never brought that brute here ! He'll end by biting one of the children. You'll see if he doesn't."

" Give him time," said Pryce. " He'll be all right. He's not used to us yet."

At last Peter turned to his dish of food and devoured it. He stalked through the open doors into the fenced-in garden at the back of the house and investigated every corner of it. That night he submitted to having his lead snapped on and Pryce took him for a walk. Pryce came home tired out. The big-boned, heavy dog had dragged him all the way, sniffing, searching for the scent of the one he loved.

After the time of anxious watching came a time of spiritless acquiescence. He allowed the children to pull him about. He stood calmly submissive while

Mrs. Pryce brushed his silky coat. She liked having a handsome dog about because it was the fashionable thing to do. She had the children photographed with him and sent one of the pictures to young Ffolkes who had it framed for his room in London. On it she had written, in large black writing, " Joan and Kenneth with their faithful friend, Peter."

She had ideas, gathered from the advertisers of dog foods, about what a dog should have to eat. She did not at all approve of what Ffolkes had told her of Peter's former diet. Now he was given only one meal a day, that of a prepared food moistened with water, and at night a small hard dog biscuit. Peter, accustomed to the rich and varied diet at Mrs. Dowling's, ate only enough of this to keep him from starvation. He grew gaunt and yet, in an austere way, more beautiful. Everyone admired him. He was : " That beautiful Scotch collie of the Pryces'." Mrs. Pryce entered him in a show. He took second prize and might have taken first had he not been so spiritless. She proudly led him about, showing off his ribbon.

At home he spent almost all his time guarding the leather chair. He would allow no one to touch it, but sat with his long delicate muzzle resting on one of the padded arms.

On one of the occasions when Ffolkes had been a guest of the Pryces' he had, to please the children, made a record on the dictaphone which Pryce had in his study. One night Joan had the idea of letting Peter hear his distant master's voice. They were all

in the room together, a bright fire was blazing in the grate.

Now came Ffolkes's voice, terribly familiar :

" Hallo — hallo, children ! How are you ? Pretty well, eh ? What shall I say to you ? Why — look here — I'll tell you — I've got a dog — a lovely dog — a Scotch collie — his name is Peter — Peter—! "

At the first sound of Ffolkes's voice Peter sat erect. He sat as though listening with his whole being, drinking in that precious voice with every hair of his beautiful coat. Then, with a bark in which all the longing of months burst its bounds, he leaped to the dictaphone, rushed round it frantically and as the voice ceased looked in consternation at the box from which it had proceeded.

There was a burst of delighted laughter from the children. Mrs. Pryce joined in with, " Well, isn't that amazing ? He remembers perfectly ! I must write and tell Mr. Ffolkes."

But Pryce observed : " I don't think it is quite fair to the poor brute. Look at him — he's half beside himself."

" Oh, Daddy, Daddy, I want to do it again ! "

" Please, please, Daddy ! " chimed in Kenneth.

" No," said Pryce. " It will unsettle him again."

" Nonsense," said his wife.

But Pryce was firm.

But he could not know what was going on when he was away. It became a favourite game with the children to let Peter hear Ffolkes's voice. The result was always the same. The terrible tension. The joyous outcry. The bewilderment. The despair. The abject creeping back to his post by the chair.

Then one day, before Peter could return to it, Kenneth scrambled into the seat of the chair and curled up there. When Peter approached he kicked at him and shouted :

" Get out, Peter ! My chair now ! "

In a flash Peter was on him, had dragged him from the chair, shaken him and stood over him, every fang showing.

When Pryce came home he found a distraught wife. Fiercely she poured out the whole story. She had had the doctor to see Kenneth and fortunately, by a miracle it seemed, he was not hurt but dreadfully shocked, poor darling ! The dog must be shot or sent away. She couldn't bear to have him in the house.

" Kenneth brought it on himself," said Pryce, pale and worried. " He must never tease him again. I'll give Peter a good thrashing and I do want you to give him another chance."

He went to the garage and got a short length of rubber hose. He found Peter in the cellar and beat him with great severity. He was left there all the next day.

When Pryce returned that evening he went to release him. He had an embarrassed, almost shame-faced feeling, as he descended the stairs. He went to where he could see Peter sitting upright in the twilight but he felt that he must be firm.

" Come here," he said, authoritatively.

Peter rose, approached him, looking him full in the eyes with a remote dignity.

They went up the stairs together.

Mrs. Pryce gave him another chance. She wanted, if possible, to keep him for exhibiting and the children had promised never to tease him again. The leather armchair had been sent away to be sold.

Peter seemed not to notice its absence. He was a different dog. Even when Joan and Kenneth, their parents being safely out of the house, put young Ffolkes's voice on the dictaphone, Peter did not turn his head to listen. He sat immovable, cold and hard. Nothing could hurt him now. He had become Peter — a rock.

REUNION

A Sequel to "Peter—a Rock"

YOUNG Ffolkes sat on the deck of the ocean liner, his travelling rug wrapped neatly about his legs, a freshly lighted cigarette between his lips and the latest crime novel on his lap. Its title, in snaky black letters on a canary ground, stared up at him : *Twice Murdered*.

But he could not get on with the book. He was too much excited, too much stirred by emotions of exhilaration and regret. He was going back to the place where he had been born and had spent all his life except the past two years, and his spirit strained forward to the old familiar scenes. Yet the two years he had spent in London had been the most full, the most expansive, of any he had known. He had made friends from whom it had been hard to part. He had found in London a new home — the great town had taken her colonial son to her heart with the simplicity of a village.

It was a man's town, he thought, looking back on London ; and there he seemed to have reached his full manhood. He felt immeasurably older and more experienced than when he had left Canada. He had been promoted by his bank to a very good post in their London office. He had done well there and now he was being returned to Canada to a still more responsible post. Pretty fair going, he thought, for a fellow of thirty.

The deck stewards came along with a trolley laden with cups of hot bouillon. As the steward gave Ffolkes his cup he remarked cheerily, " Well, sir, Canada is preparing a grand welcome for you. I've never seen finer weather."

" Glorious," said Ffolkes. And glorious was the word for it. After the coldest, wettest spring in many years, this effulgence of blue and gold, these happy waves, this flowering spray, made crowded streets, jostling umbrellas, electrically lighted offices and piles of ledgers grotesque, almost impossible.

There was something very likeable about young Ffolkes. Everyone on board seemed to know that he was going home after two years in London, that he had no relatives living to welcome him and that he was looking forward, with touching eagerness, to seeing a loved collie dog named Peter. Everyone wondered whether or not the friends with whom Ffolkes had left the dog would be willing to give him up. There was the danger that they had become too greatly attached to it.

And there was the dog's side of the question

to be considered. It would be rather rough on him to be uprooted again, after two years, especially as he was now living in a house with children. Dogs were nearly always devoted to children. The mothers on board gave Ffolkes practically no hope of winning back his dog's love without the lure of children to help him.

But Ffolkes was scarcely cast down by their predictions. The love between him and Peter had been too deep, the understanding between them too sensitive to be lost, even after a separation of two years. He pictured their reunion and in imagination felt Peter's lithe, muscular body clasped against his own, saw his wide grin showing his long red tongue and superb teeth.

He showed his own teeth in a smile of satisfaction as he sipped his *bouillon*; and the captain, strolling along the deck, dropped into the vacant chair beside him and said, with his tolerant twinkle, " Thinking of Peter, eh ? "

Young Ffolkes was abashed. He must be a nitwit, he thought, to exhibit to the world a face that could be read at a glance. He drew it peremptorily into the mould of gravity that had furthered his promotion in the bank, and answered, " Oh, well, it's very nice to be going home."

" And after all," went on the captain, " he's your greatest pal over here, isn't he ? "

" Oh, rather ! "

" He must be a beauty. Won prizes, you say. I should like to see him."

In his pride of Peter, Ffolkes's gravity became very boyish. " Why, look here," he said, " I have a photograph of him. I'll fetch it, if you like."

The captain did like. He settled his stocky figure in the chair and picked up *Twice Murdered*.

In a few minutes Ffolkes returned with the framed photograph. He said, " You can imagine I was pleased when they sent me this. It's a perfect picture of him. And those are the Pryce kids."

The captain took the picture in his square brown hands and examined it. Across it was written, in large black letters, " Joan and Kenneth, with their faithful friend, Peter." He observed :

" Attractive kids."

Ffolkes was disappointed. What the devil did he care whether or not Pryce's children were attractive ? What he wanted was the captain's opinion of Peter.

Now he had it. " He's a beauty. I don't think I've ever seen a grander head on a dog, but——"

" But what ? " demanded Ffolkes.

" Well " — the captain spoke hesitatingly — " you have talked of his high spirits and his joy in life, but in the picture he looks rather spiritless to me."

" Of course, it's only a picture. He probably hated being photographed. Most dogs do."

The lady in the chair on Ffolkes's other hand could endure her curiosity no longer. " Oh, do let me see ! What an adorable picture ! Oh, Mr. Ffolkes, it's your wonderful Peter ! "

The lady, who was mother to the most spoilt child on board, declared that Peter would die of a broken heart if he were separated from Joan and Kenneth.

Ffolkes brooded a good deal on these remarks. They somehow dulled the brightness of his anticipation. Or perhaps it was the heat and noise of the long train journey which succeeded the voyage. But when he reached the boarding-house where he had spent six happy years and where he had brought Peter as a puppy, his spirits went up with a leap. He could scarcely wait to pay the taxi driver and see his luggage into the house, he was so anxious to take possession once more of the large room at the top.

Little change had taken place there since he had left. Of the seventeen ladies — to whom he had been, as the only male guest, the centre of attraction — sixteen remained. Mrs. Forrester had gone to live with a married daughter. But, it being the summer season, most of the ladies had gone to the agreeable places where they spent the hot months. Only ugly, kind Mrs. Kane, hearty, loud-voiced Miss Hubbard and pretty, white-haired, pink-cheeked Mrs. Slee remained. These three clustered about him in the drawing-room in a state approaching bliss. They had never hoped to have him back with them. With his departure something of the glamour of living had gone. Not that the ladies were in any way dissatisfied with their lots — the days passed very happily at Mrs. Dowling's. But they had enjoyed the presence of young Ffolkes in the house and it seemed almost too good to be true that they had him back.

In his new position he could have afforded to keep

up a good establishment of his own. That might
come later. For the present he was satisfied to take
up the threads of his life as he had left it, to enjoy the
comfort of Mrs. Dowling's house and the good food
provided by her cook.

Mrs. Dowling was as handsome as ever, he thought,
as she stood smiling at him in his room after lunch.
" Now, what about Peter ? " she asked. " Are you
going to get him back again ? "

" Should you like to have him, Mrs. Dowling ?
Do you think the ladies would mind ? "

" There isn't a soul in this house who wouldn't be
glad to have Peter back," she said emphatically.
" Several of us went to the dog show last fall just to
see him. He looked grand, but he didn't seem to have
any use for his old friends, I must say. He looked sort
of haughty and don't-care. I suppose you know he
took a prize."

" Yes, Mr. Pryce let me know. What I'm afraid
of is that they won't want to give him up. But I
think I have a right to ask for him, don't you ? "

Mrs. Dowling became suddenly furious. " Give
him up ? Give him up ? I should think they would !
You just lent him to them, didn't you ? The glory
they've had in taking prizes with him is more than
enough for them, I should say."

" Well, I'm glad you think so. There were people
on board who felt that it would break Peter's heart to
separate him from the children. What do *you* think
about that ? "

Mrs. Dowling felt very strongly that the Pryces

had no claim whatever on Peter. All that young Ffolkes needed to do was to call at their house and request, politely but firmly, the return of his dog. Mrs. Dowling's establishment was waiting for Peter, just as it had waited for his master.

Ffolkes's sensations that night were that odd mingling of the familiar and the strange which one experiences after return from long absence. All about him was so familiar that he expected at any moment to hear Peter as a puppy snuffling in his basket, yet all was so strange that he felt at times that he was in a dream and would never see Peter again.

The next morning he went to the bank where Pryce was manager. He found that Pryce was attending a board meeting and would not return to the bank that day. At lunch-time he called up Pryce's house and was told by a maid that the family had gone to their summer cottage for the week-end. No, the dog had not gone with them. He took up too much room in the car.

This was splendid luck, thought Ffolkes. He had not hoped for a chance of meeting Peter alone, without the beguilement of Joan and Kenneth to come between them. He called a taxi and went straight to Pryce's house.

It stood in a curving, tree-shaded street and its front was secluded by large shrubs in white flower. A lawn sprinkler whirled its cool freshness on the grass. " By George, it's been a nice home for Peter ! " thought Ffolkes. "I wonder if he'll be glad to see me."

But he really did not wonder. He was confident of the furry torrent of love that would in a moment leap on him.

He opened the gate and strode eagerly along the brick-paved walk.

He heard a low growl, then stopped, profoundly surprised by what he thought for a flash was the statue of a collie dog sitting on the balustrade beside the stone steps. It could scarcely be real — that rigid, immobile beauty ! Then he knew that it was Peter.

He took three strides and had him in his arms. " Peter ! Peter, old man ! Glad to have me back ? Dear old pal ! "

There was no more response than would have come from the statue he had at first thought him to be. Yes, there was a response, after all — a terrible one. He felt Peter's hackle rise under his hands !

Young Ffolkes stepped backward with an air almost ludicrously crestfallen. His arms fell to his sides. His jaw dropped. " Peter," he said, softly. " Pete, old man ! You can't have forgotten me ! You simply can't ! I'm Ffolkes — Ffolkes, your old pal ! *Peter !* "

The last word was almost a cry, for now he saw that Peter did remember him ! There was recognition in those remote hazel eyes. Remembrance — but no love. They looked through him, past him, with a dignity remote and unapproachable. The hair on the back of his neck settled into place. He ignored Ffolkes.

Ffolkes gave a sickly smile. He could not comprehend how such a weaning away could have taken place in two years. The understanding between him and Peter had been so complete. Peter was so intelligent.

Well, there was only one thing for it and that was to win him back. Probably a day or two alone together would do the trick.

He tried to say comforting doggie things — Nice old fellow . . . good old boy — but the words stuck in his throat. Very quietly he took one of Peter's paws and held it in his hand, that firm muscular paw that had padded beside him many a happy mile on their holiday in the north. Peter allowed him to hold it. He looked down at Ffolkes's hand, then up into his face ; and, to Ffolkes's mind, his look held not so much coldness as a terrible and abiding reproach. What had happened ? How was he ever to find out ? That look cut him to the quick.

He went to the door and rang the bell. A smart, matter-of-fact maid answered it. Ffolkes asked her to tell Mrs. Pryce that he had called to see Peter. Then : " He seems very quiet," he remarked.

" He's always like that," the maid answered. " He's a good, well-behaved dog. But underneath he's got a mean streak. He's snapped at two or three people for no reason at all. I keep clear of him myself."

" I suppose," said Ffolkes, " he is devoted to the children."

" Oh, I don't know about that. I don't think he cares for anyone but himself. You see, he's a show dog. He's won prizes and been fussed over. I guess it's made him conceited."

New bewilderment was opening up before young Ffolkes. If only he could find out what it all meant ! If only the girl were a more sympathetic person ! Still, she seemed intelligent. He felt that if anyone could help him she could. He said :

" He's really mine, you know. At least, I think he's mine. But it must depend on what Mrs. Pryce feels about it. She has kept him for me for two years while I have been in England. I want him back most awfully. Do you think she will let me have him ? " He looked anxiously into her eyes.

She became a little less matter-of-fact. " Well," she said judicially, " I can't say. Madam is very proud of him. She likes to show him off and all that, but I do know he gave Master Kenneth an awful shaking-up once — that was before I came — and she's sort of nervous about leaving him with the children."

" Then you wouldn't say that he's very fond of the children, would you ? "

" As I've said before, I don't think he's fond of anyone but himself. He's a cold, proud dog, I'd say."

When she had shut the door, he went down the steps and stood looking at Peter. He did not approach him again. Peter sat noble-looking and remote as though carved out of stone. He looked as though the goings and comings of no one on earth could affect him. He did not give Ffolkes a glance when he returned to his taxi.

" It is ridiculous," thought Ffolkes, " to feel so awful about a dog. I expect that anyone with any sense would say that it is ridiculous. Yet I do feel awful. I feel as though the bottom had fallen out of things." He threw himself back in a corner of the taxi and gave himself up to blackness.

But later on he called himself a fool for being depressed about Peter. What he had to do was to get him back and all would be well. He was glad he had had that talk with the maid ; it was a relief to know that Peter had not given his heart to young Kenneth, at any rate.

On Monday morning he found Pryce in his office at the end of the marble-walled bank. He thought that Pryce was a little embarrassed when they met. He supposed it was due to reluctance to give up Peter. Ffolkes came straight to the point.

"I wish you would tell me what I said when I left Peter with you. I can't for the life of me remember. Did I give him to you outright ? I must just throw myself on your mercy, but I do want very much to have him back."

Everything was different from what young Ffolkes had expected. He had expected Peter to be half-mad with joy at seeing him and Peter had given him no faintest sign of love. He had expected difficulty in getting the Pryces to give him up and he met with no opposition at all. Pryce said that he thought his wife would be quite willing to part with the collie. He was too big for the city ; he was too big for the car ; and at their summer cottage he had a habit of absenting himself for days, which was very worrying. Mrs. Pryce thought she would rather have a dachs-hund. They were fashionable just now.

Yet Pryce still remained embarrassed when Ffolkes expressed his gratitude. He evidently had something on his mind and Ffolkes, with resentment in his heart, tried to get it out of him. He asked questions about Peter's life in the past two years. Pryce was noncommittal. The most he could be brought to say was that Peter had not turned out to be so friendly as they had expected and that he guessed he had given all his love to Ffolkes before they had him. Yes, he was pretty good with the children. They had had a lot of fun with him. . . . Ffolkes could take him away whenever he wanted.

It all seemed too good and too bad to be true.

" What have I taken on ? " thought Ffolkes as that very afternoon he and Peter walked through the streets on their way to Mrs. Dowling's. " How is it going to end ? Am I to have this frozen statue for a companion or am I going to be able to win him back to what he was ? " The first bitterness of his disappointment over, he was on his mettle. He would leave nothing undone that might help to bring the old prideful gaiety, the trustful affection, back into Peter's eyes.

Peter stalked now, on his leash, neither straining forward nor lagging behind but accommodating his step to Ffolkes's with disdainful submission. When other dogs approached him his hackle rose and he uttered a growl, low but so menacing that they slunk instantly away. During the long walk he gave no sign of interest in anything they passed.

The three guests at Mrs. Dowling's were enchanted

to see how he had developed. He was as beautiful as a dream, declared Miss Hubbard ; and indeed there was a strange dreamlike quality about him, as though he were scarcely conscious of what went on. Mrs. Kane remembered how she had been the one to name him and Mrs. Slee recalled how she had saved his life when as a puppy he had escaped into the street. They were rebuffed when he took no notice of them whatever, only submitting with an air of polite resignation to their fondling.

That night he slept in Ffolkes's room. Purposely Ffolkes had not taken him to it till bedtime. Now he paid no attention to him, allowing him to sense the once-loved atmosphere for himself.

Ffolkes's heart quickened its beat as Peter stood motionless but with eager eyes in the middle of the room. His sensitive nostrils quivered. He sniffed every corner of the room. Then he gave a sharp whine and turned once again that look of terrible reproach on Ffolkes.

But that was the end of it. He had weakened, it seemed, for that moment only. When it was past he was once again remote and invulnerable. He seemed buried in a reverie from which nothing could rouse him.

Ffolkes was not yet disheartened. He remembered how, on a trip to the north country, Peter had attained the fullness of his doghood. How the shallow puppy brightness of his eyes had deepened to a steady glow of pride and confidence, how he had learned, it seemed, to read Ffolkes's very thoughts !

Ffolkes made up his mind to have a like holiday

this year. He longed to see that wild and lovely country again, and his persistent hope led him to believe that in that noble solitude the wall that separated him and Peter would crumble.

He bought a car and a tent and arranged to go to the same spot where they had camped two years ago. Ffolkes felt very hopeful when he saw Peter standing foursquare to the summer wind on the seat of the car in the midst of the outing paraphernalia, his head high, his adroit nostrils sniffing the pure air.

In the northland that air swept untainted over vast tracts of virgin country. Ffolkes had forgotten the great fine sweep of it.

He and Peter seemed the only inhabitants of a new and glorious world. Ffolkes, remembering his holidays of the past two years, pitied the people of those seaside resorts who swam, paddled beach boats, and rode on surfboards, never out of sight and sound of one another. At sunset he found the very spot where he had raised his tent on the former visit. He found traces of his old fires. He found the circular stove of flat stones which he had built, where he had cooked his fish. The same settler came to bring him bread and milk and vegetables.

He was hot and tired from the long drive. He could scarcely wait to strip off his clothes and plunge into the cool lake. He remembered how Peter, after his first puppyish hesitation, had swum beside him, glorying in this new freedom and intimacy.

He ran across the sand and out into the green depths. Peter stood on the shore.

"Peter ! Peter ! Pete, old man ! " he shouted. "Come on — it's simply great ! "

But Peter viewed the forest, the lake, the tent pitched on the well-loved spot, with no more response than he had given to his reunion with Ffolkes. His plumed tail which he had used to wave extravagantly in his joy, now drooped in majestic melancholy.

As Ffolkes came dripping out of the water he said aloud, forcing hope into his voice, " To-morrow — he will be himself to-morrow."

That night he made a bed for Peter at the foot of his own couch of balsam boughs and army blankets but the collie, after sniffing it, stalked out and curled up near the dying fire.

" He is a different dog," mourned Ffolkes. " I can never win him back. He's lost."

He could not help reproaching himself for the change that had come over Peter. He felt that he should have known more about the Pryces before leaving a sensitive dog with them. But they had seemed so kind and there had been the children for playmates.

It was long before he fell asleep. The strange noises of the forest crept closer, became more personal. Yet it was no forest noise that woke him from his first sleep but terrible heart-rending howls — howls that gave voice to a despair long stifled. Ffolkes leaped from his bed and tore wildly at the flap of the tent.

Peter was sitting by the embers of the fire, his muzzle raised to the low-hanging stars, while out of his deep chest those anguished howls came in dreadful succession.

Ffolkes shouted to him. He ran and put an arm about him and stroked him. "Peter, dear old fellow, what's wrong? Lord, if only I knew what you want!"

Peter hung his head as though ashamed of his outburst and from that time their nights were undisturbed.

To Ffolkes the holiday was a failure, though the weather was perfect, the fish fairly shouldered one another out of the lake and his own body became lithe and brown as an Indian's. He made the journey back to town with a heavy heart. Peter sitting beside him was a noble figure, his full ruff as white as the foam of the lake ; but his spirit was still a prisoner in the remote world to which it had withdrawn.

One night weeks later, as Ffolkes sat pulling at his pipe, an idea came to him about Peter, of whom he found himself thinking in every spare moment. He would take him to the Pryces' house and see what his reactions were to that house and those people. He might find out something. If there was psychology for human beings, why not for dogs ?

The next afternoon he and Peter arrived at the house without warning. The maid told him that Mrs. Pryce and Joan were away for the day, that Pryce was expected at any moment. Only the little boy was in the house. Would Mr. Ffolkes come in ?

Kenneth swaggered out to the verandah at that moment, important at being the one to receive Ffolkes. They shook hands and then Kenneth took Peter by the collar and began to pull him about.

" Hullo ! " he exclaimed. " Aren't you an old silly ! Don't you know me ? "

Ffolkes's anger rose against the boy but he forced himself to grin. " I guess he's not likely to forget *you*, eh ? " he said.

" I'll bet he won't," returned Kenneth, getting astride the submissive dog.

" I suppose you and Pete had lots of fun."

Kenneth gave a grunt of assent as he joggled up and down on Peter. Then his face changed as the collie's hackle rose and he got to his feet. " Mother's glad you've taken him away," he said, pushing out his lips. " She was afraid he'd go for me again."

" Go for you ! " grinned Ffolkes. " What d'you mean, go for you ? Surely he wouldn't do that ! "

" Surely he would," affirmed Kenneth vigorously. " They had the doctor for me. I wasn't really hurt. But Mother was scared."

" No wonder ! " Ffolkes kept the grin frozen on his face. " I expect he got a good licking for that, eh ? "

Some family instinct impelled Kenneth to deny this. " No," he lied. " But he should have had a good licking with a piece of rubber hose. That's what I said."

" Of course he should ! " Ffolkes's voice grew even heartier. "What was it that made him go for you ? "

" Why — why, I just drove him off his chair. The one that was yours. The old silly used to lie with his chin on the seat. I just jumped into it and drove him off and then he went for me." Kenneth stared glumly at Peter, sitting statuesque and aloof.

" I expect," said Ffolkes, oozing geniality, " that you've had lots of fun teasing him, you and Joan. It's fun teasing dogs."

Kenneth looked sly. " Did we ! You can bet we did ! But the best fun of all was when we would put the record on."

Ffolkes looked sly, too. " Record ? " he purred. " What record ? "

" Why, the one you made on Daddy's dictaphone. Don't you remember ? You did it for us kids one night when you were here to dinner. Gosh, that was what made him wild ! Oh, it was fun !" Kenneth rolled over on the swing couch in mirthful remembrance.

" Ha, ha, ha !" shouted Ffolkes, clenching his hands. " That must have been fun ! He'd go wild, eh ? "

" Wouldn't he just ! He'd fairly tie himself into knots, thinking you were really there. Then, when he found it was all a sell, he'd slink away looking as mean as anything."

Ffolkes made hysterical chuckling sounds. " I'd give a dollar," he said, " to see that."

Kenneth looked suddenly serious. " Would you truly ? "

" Would I ? I'd give two dollars in a minute. It would be such fun ! "

" I'll do it ! I'll do it before Dad comes." Then the brightness went out of his face. " But it's no go. He never showed off properly again, not after the——" He caught himself in time.

" The licking," supplemented Ffolkes. " You see, I know all about it."

Kenneth grunted sulkily, then he said, " Well, anyhow, he's got you back now. He wouldn't care."

" He doesn't like me much now. Perhaps he'd like the voice in the box better than the real master. Let's try him, Ken. Come along ! "

He caught hold of Kenneth and pushed him toward the hall. As he felt that firm body in his hands he saw suddenly before his mind's eye the livid title of the thriller he had been reading on board ship — *Twice Murdered* — and he grinned ferociously.

" Come, Peter ! " he called. " Come along, boy ! "

In Pryce's study he slapped the two-dollar bill on the table. " There ! " he exclaimed. " Now for the fun ! "

Kenneth looked askance at the money. " I didn't ask for it, did I ? I'm not supposed to ask for money."

" It's a gift," assured Ffolkes, and Kenneth pocketed it with dignity.

Ffolkes's heart pounded uncomfortably. Peter sat in rigid attention. He knew what Kenneth was going to do. He was going to call out from that mysterious box the voice that had once so driven him to desperation. He sat as hard as iron, his nerves tense to repel the onslaught. Ffolkes had slipped out into the passage.

Now came the familiar voice :

" Hello — hello, children ! How are you ? Pretty well, eh ? What shall I say to you ? Why, look here, I'll tell you — I've got a dog. A lovely dog, a Scotch

collie. His name is Peter — Peter. He's a grand fellow, Peter is . . ."

Ffolkes came into the room. He did not just walk in but he came as though in answer to the summons of his own voice. His arms were tense. His heart pounded in his side. His own voice took the words from the machine :

" Peter ! Peter ! I've got a lovely dog named Peter. A Scotch collie — my own Peter ! "

Every hair of Peter's beautiful coat rose in an ecstasy of attention. A great change came over him. The chains of despair that had held him dropped from him, broken. His prison was demolished. He gave a succession of barks, almost savage in their release of his spirit, and circled about Ffolkes as though it were the first time he had seen him since his return. Then he leaped full upon him, his paws on Ffolkes's shoulders, almost knocking him down. Ffolkes clasped him close, and their bodies rocked together.

This was the sight that Pryce saw when he entered the room.

THE END

Printed in Great Britain by R. & R. CLARK, LIMITED, *Edinburgh.*

BOOKS BY
MAZO DE LA ROCHE

Chronicles of the Whiteoak Family

Crown 8vo Edition. 3s. 6d. each.
Set of the 6 novels in a cardboard
box, 21s.

Pocket Edition. 3s. 6d. each.
Set of the 6 novels in a
cardboard box, 21s.

(1) YOUNG RENNY

★(2) JALNA

★(3) WHITEOAKS

★(4) FINCH'S FORTUNE

(5) THE MASTER OF JALNA

(6) WHITEOAK HARVEST

★ Also supplied in cloth at 2s., and in leatherette
at 2s. 6d.

(*All prices are net*)

MACMILLAN AND CO. LTD., LONDON

BOOKS BY
MAZO DE LA ROCHE

GROWTH OF A MAN. 8s. 6d.

BESIDE A NORMAN TOWER. With
Illustrations by A. H. WATSON
3s. 6d.

THE VERY HOUSE. 3s. 6d.

EXPLORERS OF THE DAWN. 3s. 6d.

LARK ASCENDING. 3s 6d.

DELIGHT. 3s. 6d.

DELIGHT. 2s. Leatherette, 2s. 6d.

POSSESSION. 3s. 6d.

PORTRAIT OF A DOG. With Illustrations by MORGAN DENNIS. 5s.

WHITEOAKS. A Play. 3s. 6d.

(All prices are net)

MACMILLAN AND CO. LTD., LONDON